G R JORDAN

Man Overboard!

A Highlands and Islands Detective Thriller

First edition

ISBN: 978-1-914073-93-9

This book was professionally typeset on Reedsy.
Find out more at reedsy.com

Just for the sake of amusement, ask each passenger to tell you his story, and if you find a single one who hasn't often cursed his life, who hasn't told himself he's the most miserable man in the world, you can throw me overboard head first.

VOLTAIRE

Contents

Foreword

This novel is set around the highlands and islands of Scotland and while using the area and its people as an inspiration, the specific places and persons in this book are entirely fictitious. The ferry company in this respect is also entirely fictitious.

Acknowledgement

To Ken, Jessica, Jean, Colin, Susan and Rosemary for your work in bringing this novel to completion, your time and effort is deeply appreciated.

Novels by G R Jordan

The Highlands and Islands Detective series (Crime)

1. Water's Edge
2. The Bothy
3. The Horror Weekend
4. The Small Ferry
5. Dead at Third Man
6. The Pirate Club
7. A Personal Agenda
8. A Just Punishment
9. The Numerous Deaths of Santa Claus
10. Our Gated Community
11. The Satchel
12. Culhwch Alpha
13. Fair Market Value
14. The Coach Bomber
15. The Culling at Singing Sands
16. Where Justice Fails
17. The Cortado Club
18. Cleared to Die
19. Man Overboard!
20. Antisocial Behaviour

Kirsten Stewart Thrillers (Thriller)

1. A Shot at Democracy
2. The Hunted Child
3. The Express Wishes of Mr MacIver
4. The Nationalist Express
5. The Hunt for 'Red Anna'
6. The Execution of Celebrity
7. The Man Everyone Wanted

The Contessa Munroe Mysteries (Cozy Mystery)

1. Corpse Reviver
2. Frostbite
3. Cobra's Fang

The Patrick Smythe Series (Crime)

1. The Disappearance of Russell Hadleigh
2. The Graves of Calgary Bay
3. The Fairy Pools Gathering

Austerley & Kirkgordon Series (Fantasy)

1. Crescendo!
2. The Darkness at Dillingham
3. Dagon's Revenge
4. Ship of Doom

Supernatural and Elder Threat Assessment Agency (SETAA) Series (Fantasy)

1. Scarlett O'Meara: Beastmaster

Island Adventures Series (Cosy Fantasy Adventure)

1. Surface Tensions

Dark Wen Series (Horror Fantasy)

1. The Blasphemous Welcome
2. The Demon's Chalice

Chapter 01

Macleod stepped out of the small, green sports car, shaking his head, and stumbled towards the rear door of the Inverness Police Station. He swore to himself that the next time the car was going in for an MOT, he would get a taxi rather than let his sergeant drive him to the station.

'Seoras, you forgot your coat. Do you want me to bring it?'

Macleod didn't answer and simply found his bearings to the hallway of the police station and took the stairs up to his team's office. He ignored the 'Good morning' from Ross and made for his own smaller office at the end of their work area, stepping inside and collapsing in the chair behind his large desk. It took ten seconds before there was a rap at the door, and it opened. Macleod looked up and saw his other sergeant, the red-haired Hope McGrath.

'Are you okay? You're looking a bit peaky this morning.'

'That woman—does she drive like that with you in the car, or is it just me? I felt like I was on some sort of big dipper ride. Tell me, she can see those cars, can't she? She does know they're there?'

'Well, if she didn't hit any of them, I guess she probably does.'

Macleod looked over Hope's shoulder and saw Clarissa Urquhart, the sergeant who had driven him in. She was taking off her trademark large shawl but today was sporting tartan trousers. He couldn't believe the contrast in his sergeants. Young and fresh-faced Hope McGrath was steady, resolute, and efficient. On the other hand, the older Clarissa was a woman who couldn't wait to get things done. She could charge here and there and had earned herself the name of Macleod's Rottweiler for her brisk attitude.

'I take it the coffee's made?'

'Yes,' said Hope, 'as always. You want one?'

'Absolutely and apologise to Ross. I just didn't feel like I could speak to anyone coming in.' There came a shout from outside the office.

'Ask Seoras if he wants a lift home.'

Macleod shook his head at Hope. 'I'll get a taxi,' he said. 'I'll get a taxi if that car is not ready.'

'I'll drop you off,' said Hope.

'But it's not on your way.'

'No, but I'm not having you come in like this every day. You can be grumpy enough at times, without feeling discombobulated.'

Macleod lifted his eyes to Hope, shook his head, and sat back in the seat, closing his eyes again. A minute later, he heard the door open, and a cup was placed in front of him. There was no speech and the person turned away ever so quietly, tiptoeing back to the door.

'Thank you, Ross,' said Macleod.

'Pleasure, sir.'

Detective Constable Ross was the only person on the team who nowadays called him sir. It was a staple from the past, but

2

Ross said he could never get used to calling Macleod Seoras, or even Inspector Macleod. It was always sir. Apart from Hope, Ross had been the longest to serve with him out of his colleagues and was the solid core of the team. Ross made sure everything happened, while Macleod was left free to think long and deep on cases, to make the connections. It had taken him a while, but he felt he had a team now that functioned well together.

Macleod rested his eyelids for another five minutes before opening them and looked down at the paperwork on his desk. There were various things to sign off, reports to read through, and he sat looking at them for an age, before beginning. His coffee had been drunk at this point and almost by magic, Ross appeared to take the cup away and recharge it. In some ways, he felt like a manservant to Macleod, and Seoras sometimes wondered did he take Ross for granted.

He couldn't do that with the other two. If they felt Macleod was overstepping his mark, they'd tell him. Hope, professionally and calmly. Clarissa with the sarkiest of comments.

Picking up the recharged cup, he stared through the glass at his team working in the office outside. Things had been quiet for a week. There had been a couple of routine deaths to look at, but none of them had been suspicious. Times like these he had learnt to enjoy, when there was less cut and thrust, when things were just calm. In his younger days, he'd have been itching for something to happen. Nowadays, he could stay like this for the year, although preferably without the lift in to work.

Macleod watched Clarissa Urquhart pick up the phone and begin to chat to someone on the other end. He was always taken aback by her purple hair. The woman was vivacious and in a lot of ways, he'd grown to like her, but he always felt he had to watch just in case she misbehaved too much. Some people in the force didn't like the sharp comments, but then again, she was like him, edging closer to retirement. She really didn't care less about who she offended anymore. Macleod did, but not from a worry about his job; it was just his nature.

He watched the woman scribble a few notes from her phone call and then stand up and come towards his office. Almost automatically, he put his head down in his work again as the door was knocked and then opened.

'Seoras, I think I'm going to have to give you a lift again.'

Macleod looked up rolling his eyes. 'No.'

'I've just taken a call from Minchlines, the ferry company, stating that they'd sent all of the information to the Coastguard. I think they've called the wrong place.'

'How come?' asked Macleod.

'There seems to have been a number of tragedies on the ferries recently, several passengers who went overboard and whom they were unfortunately unable to rescue. It seems that the Coastguard asked for quite a few details, but somebody at Minchlines has managed to send it to us. I've tried to redirect them. Maybe you should give them a call, because I think Minchlines has got the wrong idea.'

'Will do. They operate all up and down The Minch, don't they? And just south of it.'

The Minch was a stretch of water between the Western Isles and the west coast of Scotland. The islands were served by the ferry company in what was described as a lifeline service. The crossings varied in length, but the water could be rough in the winter. Macleod had used the ferry on many occasions from his time living on the Isle of Lewis.

'I'll give them a call,' said Macleod, 'we're not doing anything else at the moment, are we?'

'If you need to get dropped down, I can give you a lift.'

'Dropped down?' queried Macleod. 'The Coastguard's based in Stornoway for that area.'

'All right, out on Lewis? That'll be a fair hike then.'

'No, it won't. We won't need to take the car out for a run either,' said Macleod, 'I'll just ring them.'

'Okay,' said Clarissa, 'but if you need a lift back tonight, just say; okay?'

Macleod didn't even start to argue. He just waved his hand and reached down for his phone. He looked up the number for the Coastguard in Stornoway and gave them a call.

The controller at Stornoway had a name that Macleod thought he recognised from his school days. James MacArthur, as Macleod recalled, was also a quality footballer and a bit of a Romeo in his day. He'd gone to the Nicholson Institute, the same secondary school as Macleod and just about everyone on the Isle of Lewis, and Macleod was sure he would know him.

'Seoras Macleod, long time, I have obviously heard about you, seen you on the news a few times, some bloody business you're involved in.'

'Indeed, James, but I thought you'd left the island. You're back over again?'

'We all return home,' said James, 'except you.'

'You don't want me to visit,' said Macleod. 'I only bring death and destruction and that's why I'm ringing. We took a call today from Minchlines, apparently about sending us all the details on various passengers that had died. Three, they said recently. I don't understand why they're ringing us.'

'Might be enforcement branch that was looking for it,' said James.

'Is something untoward happening?' asked Macleod.

'Is this official? Because I thought enforcement were going to speak to you.'

'Speak to us?' asked Macleod. 'Why would they want to speak to us? I take it these are people who have gone overboard. I thought that was their jurisdiction out there.'

'They've got a theory,' said James, 'nobody else here knows about it but I was advised in case any information came my way, so I could pass it to them.'

'What do you mean, a theory?' asked Macleod.

'Well, I'd better tell you the whole story,' said James. 'Buckle up, it could be a long one.'

'Just hang on a minute,' said Macleod and he placed his phone down and went to the door.

'Hope, come in a minute, sit down, and listen to this.'

His redheaded sergeant stood up, strode over, and took a seat on the opposite side of Macleod's desk.

'James, I've got Hope McGrath here with me to hear this. I just want a second opinion on it because by the sounds of it, this could be quite juicy.'

'Fair enough. Hello, there,' said James, 'nice to meet you, Hope. I was telling Seoras that recently we've had a number of deaths on the ferries, people who have gone overboard. Our investigation branch has been looking into it and they've been asking Minchlines for some of their documentation. We don't think the ferry company has done anything wrong at all. In fact, they reacted splendidly each time in terms of trying to rescue the people who went overboard. We also don't think that any of their equipment or ferries are out of line in any

6

way. In fact, there's a high likelihood of suicide in all three instances, but with them so close together, we decided to take a proper look at it.

'The first one happened on the ferry from Tarbert to Uig, Harris to Skye run. A man by the name of Andrew Culshaw went overboard. No one saw him go in, but he was seen briefly in the water afterwards by a young couple on the other side of the deck, who'd simply walked round and were looking off the back of the ferry when they saw him. There are some rumours that he and his wife were having trouble, but there was nothing to indicate anybody else was with him at the time.

'We don't know the method of entry into the water. We don't know if he knocked himself out or if he simply was deciding to do it, or if it was an accident. A lot is unknown at this time. That obviously was a tragedy, and we went out looking for him, spent several days with lifeboats up and down and the helicopter, but we couldn't recover the body.'

'That's not unusual though, is it? I mean the body will wash up at some point, but it's not unusual not to find them if that happens?' asked Macleod.

'That's correct, Seoras. Once they're in, if you don't get to them quick and they go under, well, it's almost potluck in some ways. He didn't have a life jacket on. Like I say, we don't know the method of entry, could have knocked himself out on the way down.'

'Where was the next one?' asked Hope.

'Sound of Mull, Oban to Mull Ferry. A narrower stretch of water, but Peter Hughes fell off that ferry. Again, he wasn't seen going in, only once he was in the water. They didn't say he was waving or indicating any form of distress. There didn't seem to be any reaction from him in the water, which is one of the reasons why we think these are possibly suicides. However, they spun around, and tried to find him. Again, they didn't succeed.'

'Very similar in some ways,' said Macleod, 'but I guess if somebody's intending to commit suicide, it's pretty reasonable that the circumstances could be similar. Maybe learnt from the first one.'

'Well, yes, because the rescue was all over the news both times. The third one we did manage to pick up the man involved. Unfortunately, we're struggling to get his state of mind.'

'Where did that happen?' asked Hope.

'Leverburgh to Berneray.'

'Where's that?' asked Hope.

Macleod almost tutted. 'That's the Isle of Harris down to North Uist.'

'They're all pretty close, aren't they?' said Hope.

Macleod took a deep intake of breath, 'Pretty close is true,' he said; 'that's interesting. What happened with this one, James?'

'Well, again, we don't know. He was simply seen in the water. It's not that big a ferry, quite hard to go in unnoticed. Although, if people were inside, which most of them were, it is possible. But you don't get a lot of blind spots.'

'Is there any connection between the three ferries?' asked Macleod. 'Passenger names and that?'

'I don't believe they think so. I haven't been running the investigation, I'm just the Controller here at the Operations Centre. It'll be enforcement and investigations that are looking into it, MAIB as well—the Marine Accident Investigation Branch. They're having a look at it, but they seem to be saying suicide.'

'I don't like it,' said Macleod, 'it's all very neat to be suicides that close together, the closeness of water and on three different ferries. How many suicides do you get annually on those ferries?'

'They're not unheard of but maybe one a year around the coast. Most people who commit suicide don't go on a ferry first. They go to Beachy Head, down south. Up here, there's fewer specific places.'

'What's your take on it?' asked Macleod.

'It bothers me, Seoras, to be honest; it really does. One of the things with our team as well is we're not used to investigating deliberate acts of murder. We look at boat infringements. We look at where people have bent the regulations or procedures on the water, and in that sense, the ferry company looks fine. We don't think it's anything to do with the ferry company; it isn't at fault. I mean, they're a professional outfit.'

'But,' said Hope, 'there's a but coming.'

'Yes,' said James, 'the repetitiveness of this is ridiculous. Could we just be unlucky? I don't know.'

'We're not busy at the moment,' said Macleod, 'I could take a look. I don't want to step on your toes. I mean, they all happened in the maritime environment.'

'They did and certainly we can pick up the rescue side of it but to investigate if something is amiss. I mean, to say something is amiss, you're talking about someone murdering people by throwing them off the back of a ferry. How? Why? I don't know where to begin with that. I'm not sure our guys do either.'

'You begin where it always begins,' said Macleod, 'with the people. Give me the phone number of your people, James. I'm going to give them a ring. I think it's worth us taking a look at this, but from the perspective of the people involved, not from whether or not anything's amiss in the maritime environment.'

Macleod took down the number James gave him before putting the phone down. He looked up at Hope.

'It's just a feeling,' he said.

'Yes,' said Hope, 'it's just a feeling but I'm getting it, too.'

Chapter 02

Macleod got the go-ahead for his investigation, both from the Coastguard and his chief inspector. As soon as he was given the case, Macleod dispatched Clarissa down to Mull, figuring if he could get her in the car as far away from him as possible, someone else might have to give him a lift to any ferry he was going to investigate.

Initially, they would speak to the two closest ferries before sending someone down to the Leverburgh ferry, which would be a much more involved trip. Macleod was aware that he was following suspicious circumstances but that he was still responsible for investigating any other deaths and murders that happened in his area, and they may need to return quickly. On that basis, he didn't want his team scattered too far and wide.

Macleod made his way down to the Tarbert-to-Uig ferry, routing with Ross to Skye and the port of Uig where he met up with the current crew during its shuttling back and forth. Macleod had agreed to come on board to spend time with the master and the various crew members.

Macleod was given a small room and advised that the crew would pass through to speak to him, starting with the master of the vessel. Ross was on board as well, taking various photographs and being shown round by the second officer while the first officer oversaw the current passage they were on.

The master of the vessel was a man in his fifties with a serious face, someone Macleod thought wouldn't tolerate many jokes and certainly didn't seem to laugh. Macleod could appreciate a man in this position being like that. Once upon a time, he'd been rather dour himself but the formality with which the man greeted him seemed a little over the top.

'We don't get many inspectors coming out to us.'

'I would think you wouldn't. Mr McGregor, isn't it?'

'Yes, it's McGregor and you're Macleod. Seems everybody knows Macleod these days; been on the news a lot, haven't you?'

'Unfortunately, it seems to more and more be an obsession with people. In the old days, we just went and solved crimes but a lot of them, they weren't on the news or they were reported at least in a half-sensible fashion.'

'Aye,' said the man, 'that's the times we're living in, but I'm a little concerned why you're here.'

Macleod stood up from behind the desk and paced his way round the small cabin. 'I won't lie to you,' said Macleod, 'I'm not here for good reasons, but I want to assure you that one thing we're not looking at is the ferry company, or particularly the employees. We have three different vessels which have suffered a tragedy with a passenger going overboard. The crew's different on each one. The boat's different. The master's different. So far, we're being told that all the passengers are different. However, a run like this, it's—'

'Crazy,' said McGregor. 'It's crazy. It doesn't seem right,

does it?'

'No,' said Macleod, 'that's why I'm here. They said that they weren't able to recover the body from your incident.'

'No,' said McGregor, 'we tried. We turned the ship around and sent out our small rescue vessels. Lifeboats came out from Portree, Leverburgh as well as being bolstered by the Stornoway lifeboat. Later on, the helicopter was out, boats that travel up and down The Minch and from all around, they were everywhere. Coastguard did a good job but looks like he went down pretty quick.'

'But nobody saw him fall overboard, did they?' asked Macleod.

'No,' said McGregor, 'but that's not uncommon. It wasn't a particularly busy run. We believe he fell overboard from the aft of the ship. There's plenty of areas that you can't actually see someone. If he's a jumper, all he's got to do is stand up on the rails and go. You can't barrier in everywhere on a ship. Most of our passengers don't want to get off until they get to the other side. That water is darn cold.'

'How likely would you be to die if you jumped off?' asked Macleod.

'Well, I would say the water's cold and if you don't know what you're doing, learn to relax, and try and float yourself back up to the surface, you're really playing with fire. It's worse than jumping into a river—you'd have much more of a chance. We were halfway over as well; we weren't even close in.'

'What's the run here?'

'About an hour and a half. Like I say, I think we were forty to forty-five minutes after leaving Uig.'

Macleod continued the conversation with the master, but the man seemed to shed very little light on the incident. He hadn't been there but had been summoned to the bridge on discovery of the man being overboard. He could talk about the search in great detail, but that wasn't what Macleod wanted; he needed to understand the deceased passenger, Andrew Culshaw. Who was he? What had happened to him? Had he been seen onboard?

Macleod awaited the rest of the crew coming through. The master had organised the crew starting with the deckhands, the senior officers, but very few of them had even seen the man. He had parked his car down below, seen briefly with his wife. Macleod knew that was where they were heading next, to start talking to the relatives of Andrew Culshaw and see if the man's mind was focused on suicide. Although Macleod knew that wasn't always the case. Sometimes suicidal thoughts come in an instant.

It was well into his stay when the canteen chef came in, and sat down in front of Macleod, wiping his hands on the apron that spread across his lap. His trousers were bold black and white squares, and Macleod wondered why the man wouldn't look him in the eye.

'It says here that you're Anders, Anders Smith. It's a strange combination of names.'

'Yes,' said the man. 'I have a Norwegian mother, a Scottish father.' The man again looked over Macleod's shoulder rather than look at his face.

'You've been the chef here for how long?' asked Macleod.

'Four months,' he said.

'Everything okay? Work going fine?'

'Work is okay.' The man looked at the door. 'I should be getting back. Help them with the service.'

'It's fine,' said Macleod, 'the master's giving you the time.

I'm sure they can run without you. You leapt onto one of the rescue vessels, is that correct?'

'Yes. That's what I have to do when something like that happens, but we couldn't find him.'

'Okay. Did you see him while he was on board?' Anders was looking at the door again. 'Is something bothering you, Mr Smith?' asked Macleod. 'You seem to be very distracted, as if—'

'Why are you here?' asked Smith.

'We're just looking into various suicides that have happened on the ferries recently, just making sure that there isn't something more untoward.'

'Why are you really here? You have my record.'

'I actually don't have your record,' said Macleod; 'tell me about it.'

The man on the other side of the table narrowed his eyes and for the first time looked at Macleod. 'I was young. I didn't know any better. I didn't mean to kill him.'

'Okay,' said Macleod, 'but you obviously did kill someone. Who?'

'It was at a boxing club. Things kicked off. I hit him with a punch. He died and they called it manslaughter. I went away for ten years, only got out two years ago. Finally got this job, so I want to keep it. I have a wife and family now and I need this job. Do you understand?'

'Mr Smith, you're not under investigation,' said Macleod. 'I'm here looking at these suicides. Did you see this man on board?' Macleod held up a photo of Andrew Culshaw.

'Yes. I see most people that come on. Most people come for either a coffee or a drink. I was serving that day as we were shorthanded. I prepared a lot of food and then I had to come through. He was getting very agitated.'

'Really?' said Macleod. 'Why was that?'

Macleod watched the man twiddle his thumbs, clearly still nervous. 'I think he was having problems with his wife as they were arguing. I was trying to find out if he wanted the chips or potatoes, and he turned around and told me to piss away off. I said, "Excuse me?" and his wife apologised for him, but then they argued again. I think their home life wasn't particularly good. He called her something—frigid, that was the word. He called her frigid. You don't call your wife that in front of people. Even if it was true, you wouldn't say it, maybe in quiet but—'

'And how did she take it?' asked Macleod.

'She was livid. She went for him, told him this, told him that.'

'She went for him?' said Macleod. 'What? Physically, like hit him?'

'No, but she put her finger right up to his face. She let him know. The whole staff, the canteen staff will tell you. The rest of the crew, they didn't see it. They don't see the passengers the way we do.'

'And what happened after that?'

'You can confirm with the rest of the crew, but we were talking about it afterwards as you do, generally, just conversation. We reckoned that they sat down for the meal but they had another row, and then he disappeared off. She stayed down below. She came back for another coffee and a bit of cake, and then we got the call.'

'Does any of the rest of the crew know where he went?'

'He was seen going upstairs, up on deck, so we believe he was up on top deck.'

'But nobody saw him go into the water?'

'No. There was a couple on the other side of the deck, we believe, from where he was. He was then seen in the water by them as the ferry pulled away from him. They didn't know it was a person at first, but it looked strange so they shouted, and it all got a bit crazy. Then the wife, she couldn't find her husband and we launched the rescue vessels. We called, "Man overboard". It was less than two minutes from him being in the water, I believe. The master, he didn't take a chance and stopped immediately. I think he told the Coastguard it was a possible man overboard, and then we confirmed it.'

'And you know the captain's actions because?'

'As I said, I went on to the rescue vessel, the small vessel at the side of the ship, which we use to go and do these things. I pilot it. That's part of my job, and I listened to all the communications on channel 16 on the radio, the Mayday call, man overboard, all that.'

'Did you see him once he was in the water?'

'We went everywhere. Never saw him.'

'Did the couple say that he was in any way indicating to them that he was in the water?'

'No, that was the thing. It was difficult for them. He didn't seem to be moving at all. He didn't look like someone that had gone in and then thought, 'Ah, help' and start waving his hands, but it's quite a fall from the top of the ferry down. He could have hurt himself on the way in, knocked himself out. The cold could have seized him. The water, you don't want to be in there.'

Macleod thanked the man for his frank discussions and once again told him not to worry, that Macleod was not trying to hunt him down for anything else. As the day wore on and many of the rest of the crew confirmed what Anders Smith had said,

Macleod met up with Ross out on deck. As he watched the water pass behind him, the sun reflecting off it, making it sparkle, he thought how delightful it looked, almost as if he could plunge in. Of course, once you got into the water, the truth of how cold it was and how high those waves actually were compared to your head, would soon become apparent.

'So, what do we know, Ross?' asked Macleod.

'Well, sir, from my investigations and the people I've spoken to, it looks like he was up here on the top part of the ferry, over here on the port side. There was a couple on the starboard side. They turned and saw him out the back, but he was on the opposite side. So, it looks like he jumped from over that side.'

'Or was dispatched on that side. It'd be easy enough to get up and down the stairs. There's a couple of ways in and out, is there not?'

'Yes,' said Ross, 'and I'm struggling to get a picture of where everyone was. The timeframe of when he goes in, it's all a little blurred. If someone did this to him, they could be back down in the canteen in no time before the alarm's actually raised.'

'They might have had something with them to do it because they'd had to have forced him up and over those railings. You don't just push someone, and they simply spin over the railings on a ferry. Do they?' asked Macleod.

'No,' said Ross, 'it's too high. It's definitely too high. He'd either have to be forced over them or he'd have to jump or—'

'You'd have to incapacitate him, to then flip him over.'

'How strong would you have to be for that?' said Ross. Macleod pushed Ross up against the railings.

'I knock you out,' said Macleod. 'Your body's lying there. I can just grab your feet and tip you over. I can't rule out suspects of weaker strength based on that.'

'To be honest, sir,' said Ross, 'it's looking like suicide. He's had a terrible row with his wife. The other couple, they didn't see anybody up and about here, and there's nobody on this ferry who was also on the other ferries according to the records.'

'I think we'll wait and see what comes back from the other ferries. I've still got that feeling, Ross. Hope's got it, too. Can't remember the last time that both of us had that tightening of the gut. Let's see how Clarissa gets on.'

Chapter 03

C larissa Urquhart was in a good mood. She had stuck it to Seoras that morning, driving him in when his car was having an MOT and had clearly rattled him. He was so sheepish with the way he drove. After all, what was the point of having a nippy sports car if you didn't use it? After taking the phone call that morning from Minchlines ferry company, Clarissa was now navigating her way down to the Oban Ferry Terminal to speak to the crew that were currently on board.

It had been over three weeks and the crew had turned around again having had some shore leave. Clarissa had to drive from Inverness, past the side of Loch Ness all the way down to Oban, but in truth, she was loving it. This wasn't big open motorways, rather a decent 'A' road with lots of little turns through some villages and towns, and with some great countryside to look at. She was in her open-top sports car, the wind was racing through her hair, and it just felt good to be alive. The only thing that was missing was a good-looking man beside her. Well, in truth he didn't have to be good looking, but he would have to be interesting and certainly a lot of fun. It was only recently she had been to the Isle of Mull when they'd investigated some murders at the airport.

Macleod has suggested that she fly down but Clarissa didn't like the idea. It was a possibility she might have to stay down this way. When they'd been on that last case, there had been a rather interesting fireman at the airport. At the time, Clarissa was part of the investigating team and she certainly couldn't have made any moves towards the man, but maybe this time she might just get a little time away.

The other thing that was delighting Clarissa was the fact that the sun was out and today was going to be warm. Of course, it wasn't summer, but it was going to be warm in the sense that the shawl might even come off at some point. Obviously not for the drive, for the wind rushing around the little car would make you cold unless you were well wrapped up. That was a small price to pay for having the joy and wonder of such a nippy little sports car.

Clarissa had broken her journey on the way down by stopping off at a coffee house and enjoying a rather nice cream tea before jumping back into her car and speeding off. She remembered the days when she didn't have such a car and as she drove past the looks would have been at her and not at the vehicle she was in. Times had changed though. She told herself that these days, men would have to see past the superfluous packaging to the quality that was inside. She told herself a lot of things these days, but in truth, she knew she was lonely.

As she drove along the winding roads, her mind flicked through the men in her life. This fireman was certainly an option and probably the only viable one at the moment. There was that guy at the gym, the workout she went to endure on two occasions a week. After all, she had to keep reasonably fit in her job. The downside to him was he was twenty years younger, and she thought he also had a girlfriend who seemed to be in the gym a lot as well. *The man was a pipe dream but at the end of the day, everybody needed their dreams to hang on to,* thought Clarissa.

Then there was Seoras. She was very fond of him, and not only as a boss, but she also knew he was very firmly attached and so decent a man, there was no way he was ever going to leave someone he had promised himself to. *Still,* she thought as she drove along, *no need to ruin a good day like this. There's a free man in Mull I might be able to get my hands on.*

The port at Oban was looking splendid and Clarissa stood at the dockside noticing the orange RNLI vessel to one side, as well as the small ferry that ran across to the isle of Kerrera. The ferry out to Mull was not the longest run, but certainly could be the most scenic as it channelled down through the Sound of Mull. If the run continued on out to Barra, you would get to see the full delight of the Sound of Mull passing up by Tobermory.

Clarissa thought she should take the car sometime, run round the islands without having to go on work business. That was the problem. In the art investigations, you seemed to get more time off in the evenings; everything wasn't so crucial, so desperate. When a murderer was afoot, you didn't feel that you could hang about; you had to keep going.

Clarissa was aware she was more and more becoming Macleod's go-to girl, the one he would send out long distance, who could operate alone. He seemed to be keeping Hope closer at hand. She reckoned this was because he was trying to train her. It was a little bit unfair in some ways, but Clarissa had no aspirations to make detective inspector, rather she thought it was unfair on Hope because the woman knew what she was doing already. She just came at things differently to Macleod.

Once on board the ferry, Clarissa met the master, a man of maybe thirty-five, who was decidedly clean-shaven. She sat down in his cabin behind a desk as he relayed to her the day of the suicide.

'It's shaken the crew up, it really has. You don't get that sort of thing too often. Sometimes yes, it happens, and you train for it. We have our rescue vessels which we launched. There were a lot of vessels going up and down the Sound anyway. With the patch of water that we were given to search, I really thought that we would be able to find him. He was called Peter Hughes,' said the man, almost as if he'd known the guy personally. 'He'd come on board with another friend, a Gerald, Gerald Lyndhurst, he was called. I remember that because the man was absolutely distraught when it happened.'

'What exactly did happen with him?' asked Clarissa.

'You can talk to the rest of the crew later on, but I've already gone through it with them and patched it together. The story goes a bit like this: Peter and his friend had come on board and after we set off, they were in the canteen. They were seen walking around the ship together. It appears at some point they'd had a bit of a to-do, an argument. In truth, the crew felt they'd seemed very close. It's not often you see two men together and think, they're probably very tight pals. They seemed to complement each other very well.'

'But they argued?'

'Yes,' said the master, 'but not a blazing row; it was very discreet, very quiet, but it was clear that they had very differing opinions. It wasn't a slanging match or anything like that; it was very precise, detailed arguments being made, but they were being made so quietly that no one could hear. One of the crew, Jenny, she was operating the coffee cabin, and she was looking straight at them. She hadn't any customers, so she was doing what a lot of us do, just fixating on the things that are going on around us. She said to me that they had the row. She said it was deep, and she thought she saw a tear on that Lyndhurst guy's face.'

'But what happened with the suicide?' asked Clarissa.

'He went up on deck, and we haven't got a big deck with our vessel, but he disappeared from sight. That's what Lyndhurst said, and we know Lyndhurst was down below. The crew confirmed that he wasn't up with him. Anyway, there wasn't too many up top either, but they saw him walk about briefly. Then the next second somebody is shouting, "The man's in the water".'

'How did the report come to you?'

'I was on the bridge so as soon as one of the crew heard "Man Overboard' Overboard," it got relayed through the comms. We stopped the vessel, turned quickly, launched all our rescue craft, but it was to no avail. A lifeboat came out from Tobermory, also one from Oban, and they were here quick, but you can see the patch of water we've got here. We had just entered the Sound. It's small—I thought we'd get him. The trouble is though, if people go down below, you don't know when they'll surface, or where. It could be miles away. The sea's got him.

'We had people up and down the shoreline, not just the Coastguard, but lots of other searchers trying to see if he'd wash up on a beach, but we haven't seen him yet. He'll probably come at some point. These things tend to happen. He'll scare the living bejesus out of people along the shore. People don't look pretty after they come out of the water, especially several months in.'

'You have experience of that?' asked Clarissa.

'Yes, a Coastguard team member for a number of years. You get sent out to recover the body. Usually it's on rocks and that; you need to have a trained team who can carry someone deceased across and give them to the undertaker or the police pathologist.'

'Did any of your crew know why the two gentlemen were on the ferry?'

'No,' said the master, 'but Jenny spoke to him when he bought a coffee and apparently, they'd won the trip. Somehow somebody was giving away trips and they'd won it and it seemed that they were more than happy to take it.'

Clarissa was brought up onto the top deck and shown by the master exactly where Peter Hughes had fallen in. She stood staring at the water. It looked cold despite the sunlight glinting off it. She looked left and right and saw that there was no road close enough on the shoreline to be able to see the ferry clearly at that point.

'How busy is the water behind us, out of Oban?'

'Well, oh, there's usually a number of boats shooting around. You've got workboats going up and down. There's the Glensanda quarry; large vessels take cargo from there. If it's rough weather, boats come through the Sound. It's a quieter way to route, but also you get a lot of sailing yachts and vessels coming out of Oban.'

'So how easy would it be to spot somebody on your ferry?'

'What? You think that somebody else could have seen what was going on? I would doubt it.'

'What about from that road over there?'

25

'You'd have to have good binoculars and have been watching. There were no reports from the road of him going overboard, from what I understand. You can check with the Coastguard, but I don't think anybody called it in from onshore.'

'What's your feeling about it?' asked Clarissa.

'Well, it's a funny one. I talked to Jenny because she really had the closest view of them, and she talked to them. I think it's suicide, but Jenny would disagree with me.'

'Can I speak to her?'

'Of course,' said the master, 'you can speak to anyone. I'll just go and find her for you. Do you want to do it up here on deck? There's not that many people about. It's a nicer place than stuck down in one of the cabins.'

Clarissa nodded, and she let the wind blow through her hair as she waited for Jenny to arrive. There was a tap on Clarissa's shoulder. She turned around and then looked down at a young girl dressed in black trousers and a crisp white shirt. She had her hair tied up behind her and Clarissa reckoned she could barely have made twenty.

'Are you Detective Inspector Clarissa Urquhart?' the girl asked.

'No, I'm Detective Sergeant. I haven't risen that far yet, but I am Clarissa Urquhart. Please, just call me Clarissa. You must be Jenny?'

'Yes,' she said. 'You wanted to know about the man who died?'

'Yes, about him and his friend, Gerald Lyndhurst. Your boss said that, basically, you were the one who had seen them the most, and probably talked to them.'

'That's true,' said Jenny. 'He doesn't want to admit it, but I think they were gay.'

'I'm sorry?' said Clarissa.

'I think there were partners. I mean, that's the thing nowadays, isn't it? The older generation don't want to talk about stuff like that, but you know, it's the thing nowadays. There's no problem with it. I think that they were partners. I don't know how close they were since they weren't lovey-dovey; they weren't putting arms around each other and kissing in front of people. They seemed to be very quiet about it, but I thought that they were a couple.'

'Right,' said Clarissa, 'but your master seems to think that it's a case of suicide. Did Peter Hughes seem to be in that frame of mind?'

'Far from it,' said Jenny, 'that's why I don't think it's suicide at all. If it was, he must have gone downhill incredibly quickly to go and jump off a ferry. The two of them seemed to be happy together. Yes, they were debating something. It was definitely a case of something that meant a lot to them, but they weren't fighting over it in the sense of being poles apart. It seemed like an ordered discussion. It was intense, very intense, but really, something that they wanted to mutually work through.'

'Do you have any idea what it was about?'

'No,' said Jenny, 'I didn't really. I get the idea, possibly if, as they were older men, or maybe if they were a couple, maybe that was bothering them. Maybe they didn't want to show that. As I say, they weren't very overt about it. It's just a feeling I had looking at them.'

'What sort of feeling?'

'That they were in love. You can see that in everybody, can't you? You can tell when a mum loves her child, you can tell when a man and a woman love each other, two women or men together. It's the same thing, isn't it? The love? That one when you realise that somebody is together? Don't get me wrong, they may have been completely platonic. Maybe they didn't live together. I don't know. Maybe I'm putting a backstory in that's not true,' said Jenny. 'The boss calls me a daydreamer. He says I sit up there in the coffee hut and just make up stories about everybody that comes, but I don't think I'm wrong with this one.'

Clarissa thanked the girl for her input before standing on the aft deck and looking back at the wake behind it. Macleod had said to her before she had left, if there was anything amiss, they'd find it in the detail of the people. They weren't there to talk about the procedures. They weren't there to realise if there was a fault with the ferry company. They were there to see if there was something hidden amongst the people.

Clarissa understood it was a modern age, but these were older men with a very modern issue. She'd need to talk to Gerald Lyndhurst. Maybe Jenny was onto something, or maybe she wasn't. It looked like the fire chief might have to wait.

Chapter 04

C hris sat looking at the lamb chops in front of him and was struggling to decide whether or not they needed gravy. They were surrounded by peas, some mashed potatoes, and some onions he'd whipped up. He'd missed lunch on the way in. Now, starting his shift in the afternoon, he was trying to eat something quickly before they would go out to practice flying.

Having previously been in the military, Chris now flew the Coastguard helicopter based at Stornoway and had enjoyed that morning out in the sunshine at home, playing with the dog. The lively hound seemed to go here, there, and everywhere, chasing a ball that many people would not want to pick up. He had also completed a short run with her. Then, having headed into work, he realised he'd forgotten to eat. As ever there was always food available, some sort of emergency rations stored at the base, and Chris was now sitting down to enjoy them thoroughly. He hated flying on an empty stomach. He knew if they got a call out, it would be even longer until he'd get to eat.

Gravy it was. Chris went over, switched on the kettle and pulled the gravy granules out of the cupboard.

'You all right this afternoon?'

'Of course,' said Chris to his colleague, and watched Dan make his way over to the small office. Chris stood looking out the window at the airport and remembered the weather briefing he'd taken on arrival. At the moment the sky looked good, but it was going to deteriorate. By evening, the weather would clag in. There was always a possibility of a haar at this time of year as well, a thick fog that surrounded the coast, and the trouble with the airport at Stornoway was that that haar tended to sweep in from one side, sometimes occasionally obscuring the base. It just slowed everything down and made flying that little bit more difficult.

Chris heard the kettle click, took the water, and poured it into the small jug with the gravy granules inside. He stirred the mixture with a spoon, realised it was thick enough and made his way back over to the plate sitting on the table. The gravy was splashed first across the chops, then over the mashed potatoes. It looked lovely, absolutely lovely. Chris picked up his knife and fork, cut off a bit of the lamb chop and placed it in his mouth. He rolled it around his tongue before chewing and letting the hot gravy fall down his throat. It wasn't a bad life after all, was it?

Chris heard the phone go. Another of his colleagues went to pick it up, but he knew what the sound meant. They were being tasked and quickly he cut up a couple of bits of chop and threw them into his mouth, followed by several large lumps of potato. He took the glass of water from in front of him, drank from it quickly and then ran through to the office to see what the call was.

'Man overboard from the Stornoway ferry,' said his colleague. 'It's just coming in to Stornoway at the moment. Let's get that chopper on the move. It's about ten miles shy of the harbour.'

Chris raced to get his suit on and then to get out to the helicopter to fire it up, while he would wait for the winchman and the rest of the crew to gather. As he did so, he gave out a large burp. Always the same; miss your meal into work, that's the day you're never going to get to catch up.

* * *

The operations room at Stornoway Coastguard was a flurry of activity. Alison had simply put on her headset after coming back from her lunch, and the first words she had heard were 'Mayday, Mayday, Mayday. Man overboard.' The least he could have done was let her get settled in. Regardless, the rest of the team had sprung into action.

The ferry was approximately ten miles from Stornoway Harbour and they'd instantly requested the helicopter and lifeboat at Stornoway to launch towards it. Alison put out a Mayday relay on the radio advising all vessels in the area, to see if any could assist. She was also talking to the ferry, which was turning around, launching its own rescue vessels and routing back to where they thought the person had gone into the water. They didn't know the method of entry and the crew were counting the passengers to ascertain if anyone was definitely in the water, for no one had seen the person enter. Instead, through one of the windows of the ferry, a child had seen someone fall quickly past them and land in the water. At the moment, Alison was also trying to get the vessel to verify that claim, but clearly it was a serious enough one that the master had decided to act on it anyway.

Alison's colleague was quickly constructing a plan of where the lifeboat and the helicopter should search, something they called a rapid response search plan. There would be more plans to draw up if these first ones were unsuccessful, and the forecast for the evening was looking like the weather was going to decline badly.

The Stornoway Coastguard helicopter called on channel 16, the main VHF channel for all maritime traffic, and it was advised to route direct to the point of entry and was given a search plan to work off from that position. It was times like these that being an operator of the Coastguard working Channel 16 became so busy. Normally it was just routine traffic, bumbling through, reporting some minor points that the vessels were passing, but when a job was on, the channel 16 position could become incredibly busy.

Alison always marvelled at how calm the services were in their response. The radio telephony switching back between the helicopter and the station, clean, accurate, precise. Then, when the lifeboat called up, she fired out instructions for it. A glance over her shoulder allowed her to see the lifeboat racing past the station making way out of the harbour towards where the incident had happened. Several other vessels were now converging, and Alison was finding it hard to keep typing up the notes that automatically went into the job record on her computer screen, noting all the information that was flowing through her ears.

Yet with all this, her heart was skipping a beat. Many of the jobs they got were routine; a yacht had broken down and you became something like the AA on the sea. But this was different. Somebody's life was in serious peril. How long could you last in the water? Well, the charts talked about lasting a day sometimes, even with it being a cool eleven degrees, but in reality, the person was unlikely to have a lifejacket on and therefore survival would be less likely.

Some twenty minutes after the fearful words 'Mayday' had come across the radio, Alison found herself finally getting on top of the job. The helicopter was into its first search, the second search was planned, the lifeboat was arriving. Other vessels were hunting, too, following the lifeboat's lead which organised them into a vast line going up and down through the area where the person had hit the water.

The ferry had called in and advised that the person entering the water was believed to be a female by the name of Daphne Walsh. Currently they were searching the vessel for her, seeing if she'd collapsed somewhere else. Maybe what the child had seen had been some bit of debris falling down to the sea, but in truth, with a person missing, and what the child had seen, it was unlikely that the two weren't connected. It was gearing up to be a long shift.

* * *

Chris was beginning to feel the effects of a long search. They'd already been out there three hours and then returned to fuel up again, before heading back out. They could see the lightboat below them, all the other vessels going backwards and forwards, but there had been no sign of Daphne Walsh. Not an item of clothing, a shoe, nothing. It was almost as if she'd gone under the water, never to come back up.

However, because the woman had entered with no life jacket on, it was hardly surprising that they hadn't seen her. The waves had started to build as the wind had picked up over the last couple of hours and they were effectively looking for a head in the water. They took the helicopter down low, trying

33

to match up the height they could be at to the distance they could see, crisscrossing the path that the boats were taking.

In the rear of the cab, Chris's colleagues were looking through cameras, checking the sea as they passed along. They also had the thermal imaging on, given that the water was cold and the body would've been hot, but as time wore on, that would become less of a stark contrast. Chris tried to keep his eyes scanning to and fro, for at this point, his colleague was flying the aircraft and not him. They took it in turns, trying to keep the fatigue away. Chris was currently wolfing down a Mars bar as he looked left and right.

From the rear of a cab, came a shout. 'Let's hold the position. I think there is something.'

'Where?' asked Chris.

'Starboard side, just down from us. Just zooming in with the camera now. Hang on, it looks like a head.'

'Get a position on that. Let's get the lifeboat over to it.'

Chris waited for the position to be relayed from behind and his colleague then took the helicopter over towards where the object in the sea had been seen. His colleagues in the rear also called the Coastguard and contacted the lifeboat so that the orange vessel was making way over to the location.

Chris looked down and could see the crew reaching out with long poles to try and make a grab for whoever it was in the water. In the rear of the cab, the winchman, who was also a paramedic, was getting ready to descend and, if needed, to whisk the unlucky woman up into the cab and off to hospital.

She doesn't seem to be moving much,' said Chris; 'this doesn't look good.'

'She wasn't moving on the camera either,' said his colleague behind him. The lifeboat crew picked the woman out of the water using long poles. Chris could see them placing her on the deck. Several of them began to work on her while the winchman called to begin his descent down onto the boat. The lifeboat was quite far out now from Stornoway Harbour and to take her back by land and then ambulance to the hospital would take so long that the winchman coming down was an obvious and simple solution to get her quickly to hospital. As Chris focused on the task of getting the winchman down to the deck, he didn't see the Stornoway lifeboat crew fighting hard for the woman's life. However, there seemed to be no reaction from there.

The winchman, having touched down on the lifeboat skirted round to the rear of the vessel and began checking the woman for any signs of life. The crew turned around and said that they thought she was dead, but as a trained paramedic, the winchman was someone who could officially call that life was extinct. After a few checks, he stood up and called it to the lifeboat crew before radioing upstairs to the cab.

Chris tried to focus on bringing his colleague back up and then safely into the helicopter before returning to the airport and touching down. Over the radiotelephony, he heard the Coastguard calling off the search, advising all the vessels that they could go on their way, thanking them for their efforts in a rather dull and sombre tone.

After arriving and doing all their shutdown checks in the helicopter and then leaving it to the ground crew to fuel up, Chris made his way to the shower and stood impassively cleaning himself down. Spending so long in the survival suit up above had caused him to sweat. Now clean, he made his way back up to sit down for a meal. He looked at the half-eaten chops, partly demolished potato and the congealed gravy now lying over the top of it all.

'I take it the ground crew is going out to get us our meal?'

'Yes. Just need to do the reports and the phone-ins,' his colleague said to him; 'make sure the Coastguard are happy, but hopefully, that's us for the day. It wasn't a pretty one.'

Chris nodded and felt a growl in his stomach. The two chocolate bars he'd had while up in the air hadn't satisfied his stomach after the missed lunch. *That's a fourth one overboard*, thought Chris. *It's almost like something's going on at the moment*. But he gave his head a shake, looked down at the meal, and threw it into the microwave. It wasn't going to taste great, but with the way his stomach was growling at him, who cared?

Chapter 05

Macleod stood watching the various officers taking statements from those onboard the Stornoway ferry. When he had arrived after the search, the local officers had cordoned off those coming off the ferry, making sure they'd take statements from everyone, trying to identify what had happened to Daphne Walsh. Her husband was also onboard and Macleod had the man assigned an officer to, first of all, help with his grief, but also then to escort him to a room where Macleod would interview him very shortly.

Macleod had been down in Skye looking to return back when he had got the call about the Stornoway ferry and had managed to jump onboard the Tarbert Ferry going back across and make his way up to Stornoway. Hope had still been back at the station, looking after things, preparing for her trip to Leverburgh, and Macleod had insisted that she continue with that rather than join them in Stornoway for the most recent event. He wanted a full picture, but that same churning feeling in his gut had continued, especially now there were four persons who had gone overboard.

Surely it was too many. Nowhere could be this unlucky. Either that, or there was an epidemic of jumping. Were people like lemmings? Did they see the idea and just simply follow it? Would these people have dispatched themselves anyway, but in a less dramatic fashion?

Macleod was struggling with the idea of it. It was a fact that throughout all his career, he'd seen many grisly murders and, in many ways, he'd begun to understand the mind of the murderer. Suicide was different and something he really did struggle with, the idea that life could get that bad. Of course, for some people it did, and for some people, it was just a medical situation that their mind went off on a tangent. It was still a subject that caused him a degree of bewilderment, despite his wife's own tragic demise in the cold waters off Lewis.

It didn't help that when he was brought up within the Calvinistic church, the idea of suicide was seen as an affront to God, something that meant you could lose your place with your Maker and whatever life was to follow. The idea of that sitting with predestination was something that Macleod always struggled with and nowadays, he just tried not to think about it. He'd seen so much, especially in these latter years, that the earlier teachings that had been given to him at times seemed hollow and certainly incorrect on occasion.

Jona had also been dispatched, looking to pick up the later Uig ferry. She was debating whether or not to send her team over that way while she flew over on the plane to do some initial studies. Macleod had encouraged the latter, but now as he stood watching the various constables under Ross's supervision making notes and pulling together what had actually happened on board, he wished his whole team were here. He found it hard when the team was split up, all in different directions.

It could have been worse for he still had Ross with him. The man could organise anything, and if Macleod was ever fortunate enough to have a daughter, though that seemed highly unlikely, Ross would be brought in to organise the wedding. The man's attention to detail was phenomenal in the height of a mountain of work, something that Macleod wasn't good at. He was the muller, the man who sat back looking at the overall picture and finding the details fly out to him. Ross was knee-deep in detail.

Macleod had taken a call from Clarissa, who was now going even further on her travels, and he was surprised when at the end of her call, she almost gave a note of concern. Was he all right without her or Hope? Macleod had said that Ross was here, but he did get the feeling that he was some sort of geriatric to be looked after. He put it down as concern rather than any obvious deterioration in his physical attributes, but that was the conundrum about Clarissa. For all that she turned round and took the mickey out of Macleod, there was a deep underlying concern that worried him, more so when he thought about it, but it made him smile. He really was getting soft.

'Sir, we've gone through just about everyone. I'm still pulling the statements and looking, but you're not going to like it.'

'Let me guess. No one about to see her?'

'That's right. No one saw her between when she went to the stairs to the top deck until she disappeared off it.'

'Do you find that strange?' asked Macleod. 'Somehow, we have four people jump off ferries and nobody sees them until they're in the water. Tell me, Ross, if you were committing suicide, would you be worried about somebody seeing you go in? Would you not be more focused on simply getting on with it?'

'They may not want somebody to see them just in case they get rescued,' offered Ross.

'All four of them? You don't think it's some sort of a club where they actually take notes beforehand how to do it?'

'No, sir. I think you may be stretching it with that one. However, I do have Mr Walsh in the interview room back at the station. I think we should really get to him. The man needs some rest. Heck of a tragedy for him.'

'Indeed,' said Macleod. 'You're going to tell me they were seen rowing, aren't you?'

'Yes, they were,' said Ross. 'Numerous people mentioned her when I showed her picture. Apparently, she was quite loud and vocal, stormed off from them. One person said she slapped him, hard.'

'Do you think Jona's going to come up with something? I mean, when bodies go into the water like this, it must be quite hard to work out sometimes what happened to them.'

'You really need to talk to her about that, sir,' said Ross. 'If you don't mind, I need to get on with these statements, try and pull them together.'

'Do these ferries have any CCTV?' asked Macleod.

'There's occasional bits around the port and that. Do you think we should do a canvas with it? See if the same person turns up?'

'It can't hurt, can it? Although if this was a murderer doing this, I doubt they'll, A, use the same name, or B, look the same each time they come on board.'

'Well, they certainly haven't used the same name. I've been checking through that already. I'll go through the Stornoway incident and see who was on board, but to be quite frank, they don't have to show their ID. You book the ferry. You can go on as a guest and book the ferry, so there's no need. The card might be the one. We'll trace the bank cards. Although, if they're smart about it and they've managed to obtain a bank card in the correct name, well, then I guess they could pay for it. You wouldn't know until it was stolen.'

'All good lines of attack, Ross. Get on to them because at the moment, I feel we're struggling. It may be we just have four unlucky tragic incidents. Four sad people that felt life was no longer worth living, but somehow, I'm beginning to doubt it.'

Ross showed Macleod over to the police car where a constable drove him round to the local station. He made his way quickly to the interview room to see a man sitting with his hands on a table and staring straight ahead, eyes full of tears.

'Sincere apologies for keeping you waiting, if I have,' said Macleod. 'I'm Detective Inspector Seoras Macleod. My sincere condolences, Mr Walsh. It must be quite a shock for you.'

'To a point, yes. You see, it's not been easy with Daphne.'

The man was dressed in a brown leather jacket and a shirt that was looking highly distressed at this time. Macleod noticed there was a coffee stain on one side, but also noted the man had taken his shoes off while waiting.

'Sorry, I hope you don't mind, but it's just that my feet swell when I get agitated. The shoes become tight. I did say to the constable, but he didn't mind.'

'Of course not,' said Macleod. 'But you said it was not much of a surprise. Why is that?'

'Daphne. I think she lost it. I've tried really hard with her. I did. We went to counselling and everything. I came home one day and there she is, some kid.'

'Kid?' said Macleod. 'What do you mean?'

41

'I don't mean a child or in that way. A kid, he must have been maybe nineteen and there's Daphne on top of him in our bed. When I asked her what she was doing, she just laughed, and she went like this all of a sudden. Over four or five years we had this, and then we thought she was getting better, and everything was okay, and then I came home and there's another kid. She'd take herself off to nightclubs. She's forty-six. We don't go to nightclubs at our age. She'd dress herself up and I tell you, Inspector, you didn't want to see your wife like that. Everything just saying, "Here I am. What do you want?" When I'd tackle her on it, she'd get angry, violent, said I didn't love her anymore. Said I couldn't see how she was. She said she was as good now as she was a teen. I think she lost her mind; I really do.'

'Did she give any indication at any point? I'm sorry for asking this, it is delicate, but did she give any indication at any point that she would be potentially looking to take her own life?'

'Nothing,' said the man. 'Nothing. She'd just bought tickets for a concert. She bought two. She told me that she wasn't going with me; she was going to take somebody she'd pick up in a nightclub and she slapped me here, right on the ferry.'

'A row? What was the row about?' asked Macleod.

'She was looking like a complete tart. Skirt was up to wherever, everything else half hanging out. I mean, she looked like a dog's dinner. Don't get me wrong, Inspector. I have no problem when she was that age and wearing that sort of thing. It was great, but now, I don't go back to wearing my tight leather trousers, I don't have my shirt opened with a medallion trying to look like something, some sort of sex symbol. That's gone. I'm older now. Comes to us all. She wouldn't accept it and I told her on the ferry. I lost it. I'd said to her, "Look, you are just an old piece of meat in a glitzy outfit." I know that was harsh, it's cruel, but it gets to you. I know the two I found her with haven't been the only ones she's been with. The doctors, they think she's gone a bit as well, lost it. She certainly wasn't seeing straight.'

'But you were getting help,' said Macleod.

'Yes, and you think it's going well and all of a sudden, out she comes wearing whatever, taking whoever to bed and not giving a toss about me. I just lost it today. Sorry. Then she went and...'

The man's head dropped into his hands, and he began to cry. Macleod held his composure for a moment, giving the man time to let his pain flow out through the tears he cried.

'Can you just enlighten me on the movements of your wife, and of yourself, from when you came on the ferry?'

'We parked down below. Both of us then went up on deck. I went down, got myself a drink and that. She followed and wanted a double whiskey, which I brought her. Anyway, then we're standing in the top lounge watching the boat sail across the Minch. Halfway across . . . , in fact, not even that, earlier than that, she's over to some kid laughing and joking with him. It was embarrassing. You could see people looking, so I told her to get back and to stop it, and that's when it all kicked off and I called her an old bag of meat.

'She stormed out, but not until she'd caught me with a couple of blows across the face, and that was it. I didn't see her again after that. The next I know, I saw the helicopter arrive and they're saying that somebody had gone overboard. The boat's turned round. I didn't think it was her at first, but then they started asking where everybody was, so I went to find her, and she wasn't there. She just wasn't there. I should've kept a tighter rein on her, Inspector. I should've held onto her. I should've . . . ,'

'And what would've happened then? She would've hit you more,' said Macleod. 'We all make our own decisions, choose our own actions. I'm very sorry for your loss, Mr Walsh. I may need to talk to you again, but I think I've got the basic gist of what happened. The best thing for you to do at the moment is to be left to have some time on your own. The constable who's been with you so far will stay as long as you need. I realise you're away from home, so I believe there's been a hotel room booked for you. You need to get some sleep. Then you can decide what you're doing, whether you want to get home. Is there anyone at home for you?'

'My brother will come,' he said. 'It'll take him a day or two to get up from England, but he'll come. Can you thank them, Inspector?'

'Thank who?'

'The lifeboat. The people in the helicopter, everybody that came out. At least they brought her back to me. At least I can say goodbye.'

'I will do,' said Macleod.

He watched as his young constable came in and took the man from the room. He didn't envy the constable's position and Macleod had been uncomfortable for the short time he'd been with Mr Walsh. In his line of work, Macleod was often with people who were bereaved, but he didn't have to stay with them. He simply interviewed them and went. The officers who stayed, they sat through all that pain. He admired them, but it wasn't something he could do himself. Of that, he was sure.

44

Chapter 06

Hope McGrath had boarded the flight that took her to Stornoway and then down to Benbecula, the middle isle of the Uists. From there, she picked up a hire car taking it from Benbecula in the middle isle to North Uist at the top of the three islands. It was connected to the Isle of Harris and thereby up to Stornoway by a small ferry run by Minchlines that set sail from Bernera, arriving in Leverburgh and crossing Sound of Harris. Hope had managed to find the master who had been on that day. He lived in Borve, right beside where the ferry came in.

When she'd been in Stornoway and in Harris, Hope had driven across many single-track roads, but her journey from Benbecula up to North Uist, although it had taken in some amazingly scenic vistas, was one that frustrated her. Unlike Macleod, Hope was more used to carriageways where cars passed easily, side by side. Here on the trip up, there were many single-track roads, and then causeways, and she found herself having to be alert to watching for traffic coming in the opposite direction.

Hope was also having difficulty finding the house of Ian Angus MacDonald and drove around Borve several times before stopping and asking someone. This made her at least ten minutes late.

The house was set off the road with a small track leading down to an abode that Hope thought could only hold one or two persons comfortably. As she approached, she saw a man inside with welding gloves on, a cylinder behind him, and about to don a mask. Two bits of metal were laid on the table in front and Hope was struggling to work out what he was building.

She stepped out of the car, thought about getting her jacket but decided against it and called over to the man.

'Would you be Ian Angus MacDonald?'

The man put down the mask that he'd been holding up to his face and turned around and looked. 'Aye. Who would you be?'

'Detective Sergeant Hope McGrath. We spoke on the phone.'

'We did, didn't we?' The man was much older than his voice gave away, Hope placing him possibly as someone heading towards retirement.

'Do you work for that Macleod fellow?'

'I do,' said Hope. 'Yes.'

'They want to put you on the telly then, not him. Inside, come on.'

Hope, for a moment, felt she should be offended in what seemed to be quite a sexist remark from an older man, but inside she actually felt quite good about it. She was struggling at times to see herself leading the team, and although the man's intention had obviously been to praise her looks, she allowed herself to take it a different way that she should be in the leadership role. The man, however, did not turn back. He simply left his front door open, meaning Hope should follow.

46

Once inside, he made his way down a hallway, opened the door to the kitchen, and pointed to the table.

'I don't suppose you ever have a dram, especially if you're on duty.'

'No,' said Hope. 'I can't, but thanks for the offer.'

'Well, just don't stand there, have a seat. I can do you a cup of tea, or a coffee, or something stronger if you really want it.'

'Please,' said Hope, 'that'd be great, just a coffee.'

She sat down at a double-leaf table that only had one side pulled out. There were two chairs, one large and one barely more than a stool with a very faint back on it. She took the stool-type chair and watched as the man pottered about with a kettle before taking a jar of instant coffee out. Hope looked at the brand and nearly spat, but beggars couldn't be choosers, and in truth, she was parched after her trip.

'So, you're the master of the Harris to North Uist ferry,' said Hope. 'How long have you been doing that?'

'Longer than you can imagine,' said the man, 'or maybe not,' laughing. 'It's nearly been thirty-five years though. That's a tricky wee stretch of water. It's got currents going here, there, and everywhere, but once you know it, it's not too bad. I mean our ferry is just a very basic roll-on, roll-off. We don't take that many cars. Enough. The trip's only an hour back and forward. You have to watch the tides. Hence, the sailing times can change. In really rough weather, well, we don't go.'

'Have you had many people go overboard in your time?'

'Well, a couple, but this was a bit different.'

'In what way?'

'Well, I think it's two we've had before. One of them was a kid whose parents should have known better. The kid was climbing up on the rails and fell off. We got him. The other one was a suicide attempt, but she was making such a noise that I think she wanted to be recovered and we got her. This is the first one on this stretch that's died.'

'What happened exactly then, from your point of view?'

'Well,' said the man, placing the coffee in front of Hope, sitting down on his chair, and pulling it close so that Hope felt his knee touch hers, 'it was just a normal run. I was up top piloting the vessel and the first I knew of it, one of the other boys shouts, "Man overboard." Of course, you stop, you put the call out to the Coastguard. We turned around and started our search. We got the new inshore lifeboat over at Leverburgh which came out, various other vessels, but we never saw anything. Not for a while anyway.'

'No? What do you mean "not for a while"?'

'Exactly what I said. For a while, we didn't see anything. Over forty minutes, the helicopter's out, then the lifeboat saw a body briefly come up and then down, and then fifteen minutes later came right past our own boat. Lifeboat got over, picked the corpse out of the water.'

'The name was Fred Martin; is that correct?'

'Yes. It looked like a suicide. The local police guy came up, he did a bit of digging, more than me. I mean, there's nothing we could do but the usual investigation and statements we had to make for the MAIB, the Maritime Accident Investigation Branch people. In truth, there was little to be done. Very sad though.'

'Was there anybody with him at the time? It doesn't say so in any reports.'

'No, he was on his own and we had to take the car off afterwards. That wasn't easy. Eventually, they broke into it, and I managed to free the handbrake. Breakdown guy came and pulled the car off. If you want to know more details about him, you need to go down and talk to Alan, the local constable. I think he's off duty today.'

'You know him well?'

'Well, yes. He came up here once in pursuit of someone. We talked, met, and yes, we share an interest in the boats. I helped him with his. In fact, why don't I take you over there?'

'I'm sure if you give me the address, I can do it,' said Hope.

'No, it'd be no trouble, honestly. I don't get that many visitors. It'd be a delight to take you there.' Hope watched the man stand up, finish the dram he had in his hand, and then stand behind her, taking her stool away as she got up. She wasn't quite sure how to take it because she should have been the authority figure. In some ways, the man was quite charming.

Hope made for her car, and Ian Angus sat down in the passenger seat before pointing her down the road. They travelled all the way back across into North Uist and made their way round to a place called Sollas, which had a long stretch of beach.

'They used to land all the private planes in there when they had a big rally. Some guy out of Stornoway came down; he organised it. I don't think he's around anymore. If you continue along the road past that, we'll get to Constable Alan McNair's.'

Hope continued to drive, and the track got even rougher than normal, but she found a house sitting beside a small inlet where the water flowed close by. She could see a boat sitting on the water, tied to a makeshift pier. As she switched off the car engine, a man appeared from the house. He was younger than Ian Angus, somewhere in his thirties, and over his shoulder she could see a young woman with him. Ian Angus exited from the car, waving towards him.

'Alan, sorry to bother you. This here is a detective. She's called Hope. She's come to talk to me about that suicide we had on the boat. I said you knew more about him than I did.'

'Grand. I did put a report in, the initial one.'

Hope, again leaving her jacket in the car, walked over to Alan McNair and extended her hand. 'Detective Sergeant Hope McGrath. Pleased to meet you.'

'Macleod. You're the one that works with Macleod.'

'I was telling her she should be the front person,' said Ian Angus. 'Better looking than that Macleod.'

Alan shot him a look. 'We don't talk like that anymore, Ian. I told you before you need to be careful.'

'She a good-looking woman. Just letting her know.' The man turned past Alan and gave a wave to the woman standing behind him. 'Hey, Alice, how are you? Another good-looking woman.'

Alan rolled his eyes, staring at Hope. 'Sorry,' he said. 'He doesn't mean anything by it.'

'I don't think he does. It's okay. It's not the worst comment I've ever had.'

Alan turned and showed Hope to the front door, where she shook Alice by the hand. Inside, they sat around the kitchen table. Hope noticed that Alice poured Ian Angus a large dram, whereas Alan joined Hope and his wife with a coffee.

'The guy was called Fred Martin who went in. I've read the report, and you say, Alan, that basically, he seemed to have jumped off.'

'That's correct. No one actually quite saw him. We don't know the method of entry, whether he struck his head or whatever, and knocked himself out. It could've explained why

50

he wasn't waving.'

'Do you know anything else about him—why he would have jumped?'

'After the initial investigation, I sent that report off, but just out of interest, I tried to make some contacts. Turns out that Mrs Martin had actually committed suicide a month previous. The couple had attended counselling and it was Fred Martin's brother who told me all this. Apparently, it seemed that it was a bit of a rough relationship; he cheated a lot with younger women, but she was besotted with him. They'd won a trip to come up here. Apparently, Fred had thought this would be a great chance to get together, but she committed suicide before the trip. That's a month previous, so the man decided to do it anyway. Not surprising then that he jumped.'

'When you say it's not surprising, is there any definitive proof that he did from the persons on board?'

'I spoke to some of them, but nobody actually saw him. He was only reported as overboard. Once he'd gone into the water, he was spotted by a member of the public at the aft of the vessel. So, the answer to your question is no. There's no conclusive proof that he jumped. It's just presumed. Why are you asking?'

'I'm sure you're well aware, Alan, that there's been a number of incidents of people going overboard recently off the Minchlines ferries.'

'One just recently in Stornoway. Do you think there's something untoward going on?'

'We don't know, but the spate of incidents is giving cause for concern. As I understand it, the Maritime Investigation Branch, the Coastguard, they all seem happy with the way the vessels are operating. It just seems a bit crazy to get that many suicides, that close together, all with very similar modus operandi.'

'Well, that's true,' said Alan. 'That's definitely true, but in this case, as far as I'm concerned, it definitely looks like suicide.'

'Quite something though,' said Hope, 'to follow up on a journey he made with the wife and then to go and end it all. Maybe it got too much for him, or maybe he planned it. Yes, well, I better get on. See where the boss wants me to go next. Thank you for your time, everyone.'

'You get off,' said Alan. 'I'll give Ian Angus a lift back over.'

Hope saw Angus' face drop. 'It's fine,' she said. 'I'll run him.'

The trip back over to Berneray was not that long, but the man made three offers of dinner for Hope and then told her that if she was passing by anytime, it wouldn't be a problem to find her somewhere to stay. As she dropped him off at the house, he turned, gave his hand to her, and when she shook it, he leaned forward and kissed her on the cheek.

'I hope you didn't take offense in that,' he said. 'It's just, well, yes. In my day that was normal. It's been an absolute pleasure to meet you.'

As Hope drove away, returning down towards the airport, she realised she needed somewhere to stay that night. In her head, she thought Ian Angus was innocent. She liked the compliment he gave her, but something else in her said there was no way she was staying anywhere in his house. As she continued to drive down towards Benbecula, it set Hope wondering. How these days do you tell the difference between the kind, sweet old man who was a little bit taken with her, and someone who had much darker intent?

Chapter 07

Macleod had spread his teams far and wide and he now wanted to make sure that he could pull together all that they'd found out. In that regard, he had called a conference call for that evening and was sitting in his hotel room with Ross beside him, awaiting Jona's arrival. The woman had made it over earlier that day. Having set up her temporary morgue at the hospital, she was hopefully coming with some news for Macleod. One of the problems they had at the moment was that there was no conclusive proof that anyone had been killed. So far, all they knew was people had entered the water by unknown means and a feeling in Macleod's gut that this number of suicides was too much to be true. He watched as Ross took the kettle and poured himself and the inspector a cup of coffee each. The constable then sat down and started fiddling with Macleod's laptop.

'I don't think you've opened the call up yet, sir.'

'You just do what you have to do,' said Macleod, 'you don't have to tell me I'm rubbish at it in the process.'

'No sir, of course not.' He watched Ross sheepishly begin to work away, then Ross turned around to see Macleod smiling at him.

'I know I'm rubbish at it,' said Macleod, 'I'm just glad you're here.' Macleod sat and watched the screen until a sudden vision of purple hair appeared. There was no face with the hair. Macleod heard Ross tell Clarissa to sort her camera out. For a moment, Clarissa's chin came into view, before finally her full face. Then Hope's image appeared in a small box in the corner.

'Good, you're all here. Just waiting on Jona to arrive. I hope everyone's okay.'

'I had an offer to stay the night at someone's,' said Hope, 'but I turned him down.'

'Wish I'd got an offer,' said Clarissa. 'I didn't even get to see a man who might have made me an offer.'

'That's a bit of a pain,' said Hope.

'Who are we talking about?' asked Macleod. 'You're on work here, not a jolly.'

'Leave her alone,' said Hope. 'I'm sure you'll get back to Mull sometime, Clarissa'

'Mull? What are you talking about, Hope? Why is she going to Mull? Who's in Mull?'

'That's the trouble with you, Seoras. When you're on the case, you see nothing else. It's a wonder that Jane stays with you.'

Macleod went to reply but actually, there was some truth in that statement. He had thought that for a while but Jane was still with him, so he didn't argue.

There came a rap at the door and a rather bedraggled Jona Nakamura made her way into the room. The woman was in a pair of jeans and a t-shirt, and her hair, rather than being tied up, hung around her shoulders. Even Macleod could see the weariness in her face.

'Are you okay?' asked Macleod.

'Let's just get on,' said Jona.

'Only if you're okay. I mean, if you've got the rest of your team here, they can join, take this if you need to go and do something. Take a rest.'

Macleod realised he was rambling at the end of the sentence. It was one of those things. Why was Jona tired? Was there something specific? Was it that time of the month? Oh, of course he can't say that. It was always the way, wasn't it? He always wondered was that it? But if he was saying it, he was somehow implying something. That was never his intention; he just wanted to know if she needed a rest.

'I'm fine, Seoras; let's get on.'

'Right. Well, let's start with Jona then from today. I haven't heard anything, so this is the first report.'

Jona gave a brief wave to Clarissa and Hope on the camera before turning and looking at Macleod. 'Right,' she said, 'I've examined Daphne Walsh and found some interesting things. It appears that she was incapacitated before she went into the water.'

'How do you mean?' asked Macleod.

'Well, her neck broke hitting the water. But then, and this took a while, I discovered she'd been injected; ketamine.'

'That's the stuff they use for date rape, isn't it?'

'Yes, but this is in a serious quantity. Highly likely she'd have been immobilised.'

'Immobilised?' queried Macleod. 'Are you sure?'

'Oh, yes,' said Jona, 'I'm sure, she was immobilised.'

'Then how did she get in the water?'

'Well, that's up to you, detective,' said Jona. 'I'm telling you she was immobilised. She could not have got into that water

55

by herself, but it also explains why, when she goes in, she's not waving for help and why she disappeared down quickly. They won't struggle; if they are lucky, they might float. However, her neck's broken. I think it's from the impact of the water. I can't find any markings indicating the neck was broken by a person. It looks like it was by an impact.'

'Could somebody have struck her?' said Macleod.

'You wouldn't strike somebody and then inject them,' said Jona, 'that would be quite messy. Also, to be hit with a force that broke her neck there was liable to be surface damage if they were using an item. The water being what it is, you don't get the same impact on the skin. You don't get any cut. It's just a simple straightforward break of the neck.'

'So, she was murdered,' said Macleod.

'That's what my judgment would be,' said Jona.

'Okay,' said Macleod. 'Hope, what about your man?'

'Fred Martin? It looks like a case of suicide. His wife died a month before, but they were in counselling. She was a bit put upon. Apparently, he seemed to have a sex addiction with younger women and was doing the sly on her all the time. He was only on the ferry because he'd won a trip. They'd planned to go on it, but she killed herself a month before it. He went anyway and then seemed to jump in the water, too.'

'Any indication he was immobilised?'

'Not from statements I've got but I haven't checked the body.'

'And you won't,' said Jona. 'I had a look for pathology reports on these bodies and Fred Martin was already cremated. They didn't do an investigation on him and in truth, even if they did, to find a needle mark you'd have to be looking. I was extremely thorough because this was the only body we had.'

'Blast,' said Macleod,' and the other two are still in the water somewhere.'

'It does kind of put an awkward spin on it,' said Hope.

'Then we have to do it the other way. We have to go digging and we have to find out who these people were, all about their lives. Hope and Clarissa, we're going to need you to dig into the three previous victims. Andrew Culshaw, where was he from?' said Macleod, scrabbling through notes.

'Derbyshire,' said Ross without even looking.

Macleod stared across at him. 'Does it just sit in there soon as you read it?'

'Well, I did think, sir, where people might need to go next. Derbyshire.'

'Hope, I want you and Clarissa to get down to Derbyshire. Go and speak to his wife. Find out what was going on within that relationship. See if there's anything untoward.'

'Okay, I'll get the plane over tomorrow down to Glasgow. If you could pick me up from there, Clarissa.'

'Not a problem. Just make sure you bring something for your hair. We're taking the little green machine.' Hope nodded and then saw Macleod's look of horror.

'I'm quite happy for the pair of you to hire a car to get down.'

'Nonsense, Seoras. I've got the car with me. It'll be nice and quick. Hope's not as fuddy-duddy about cars as you are.'

There was a silence.

'Fuddy-duddy,' said Macleod, 'just in case I don't feel old enough; fuddy-duddy.'

Macleod heard a snigger from beside him. He turned to see Ross looking the other way.

'Can I just remind everyone, we're now in a murder investigation? So down to Derbyshire first. Don't hang about either. Ross and I will tidy up this one because this is where we can get the most evidence from. We know we've got a killer on board here, so we'll get into the passenger manifest, see what's going on. We need to run plenty of cross-referencing on this. Four different instances. Let's not be afraid to understand that one of them may even be a suicide but see what we can find out about the others.'

'Once we're in Derbyshire and complete, we'll go and see Gerald Lyndhurst then,' said Hope. 'I doubt there's any point going down to see anyone associated with Fred Martin. I kind of got the lowdown from a Constable Alan McNair. He said that he'd already contacted people down there to get a fuller story, and to be fair, I think he has done. There's no wife to interview. They were in counselling so possible we could find out who the counsellor was, maybe get more information that way.'

'Very good,' said Macleod. 'I know this seems a strange case. We haven't exactly arrived at a body. We've come a roundabout route to get there but this doesn't change things. If we do have a murder, we've always got the idea that they can murder again.'

'Have we thought about putting the ferries on alert?' asked Hope. 'If we reckon there is an actual murderer on the go, maybe we need to advise them, keep people off the decks.'

'That might be the worst way to do it,' said Macleod. 'If there's definitely nobody on deck, our killer might get free licence to lob them overboard. The more eyes you have, the lower the risk of it occurring again.'

'Not sure I agree on that one, Seoras,' said Clarissa.

'Either way, I'll talk to Minchlines,' said Macleod. 'Make them aware they've got a murder with this case. Tell them what we're doing but we'll keep it quiet, talk to their chief exec and their operations manager. It'll probably be the easiest way to run this. We don't want to panic people. These ferries are about to get busy, summer coming in. They're going to be booked out and the last thing we need is a panic on our hands. I'm sick and tired of being on the media,' said Macleod.

'Indeed,' said Hope, 'I had a guy today, say to me, 'Do I work for Macleod?' You really are the pinup boy, Seoras.'

Macleod gave her a stare. 'I was going to feel sorry for you in that car, but do you know what? No.'

'So, shall we run through the plan again, sir?' asked Ross. 'Just to make sure we all understand it.'

'Absolutely,' said Macleod. 'Tomorrow, Hope flies to Glasgow, down to join Clarissa. They make their way to Derbyshire; interview Marie Culshaw to find out everything about the death of Andrew Culshaw. From there, they'll need to go and speak to the friends of Peter Hughes to check out that situation. I guess his friend Gerald Lyndhurst is the person we start with. Meanwhile, Ross is going to go through trying to ID everyone who's come on the ferry to Stornoway and we'll try and match up passenger lists. We'll see what CCTV we've got. There's bound to be some on the ships as well, just to see if we can find a common person.'

'It's going to be quite an effort, Seoras,' said Clarissa. 'If you're going to do four murders like this and you don't want to be associated with being on the passenger list, you're going to have to change your passenger name, you're going to have to book it with a different card. You're also going to have to get a different car each time. If we're quite serious about there being four murders here, and I realise at the moment we can't confirm that, we're talking about someone who's got serious planning abilities. Someone who's possibly got a bit of money, who also understands how to use ketamine properly, how to administer it, and has got the strength to throw somebody overboard.'

'I don't think they're going to have to be that strong,' said Macleod. 'These people are incapacitated.'

'And like a dead weight,' said Jona.

'But if they get them close to the edge,' said Hope, 'these ferries, it's not easy to toss somebody over, is it? And if you're beside them when you've been injected and you collapse, surely, they're going to lean up against the railings. You could grab their feet and tip them. Maybe that's why Daphne went in headfirst, broke her neck.'

'It's a long fall,' said Jona; 'you could rotate. That's not a guarantee.'

'Fair enough,' said Hope.

'Right,' said Macleod, 'we'd better get to it. Ross and I have got a bit more work today. You two get to bed, and, Jona, go get some rest.'

Jona nodded and left Macleod's room and he switched off the conference call. As Ross went to leave, Macleod looked over at him.

'Do you know what's up with Jona?'

'Well, I can't be 100% accurate, sir, and maybe I'm not the best person to look at these things but I think she's pregnant.'

'What?' said Macleod. 'How is Jona pregnant?'

Ross stood and looked at Macleod for a moment. 'Do you want to clarify that question, sir?'

'I know that bit of it,' said Macleod. 'I didn't think she was seeing anyone.'

'No,' said Ross, 'and that's why I'd leave it.' Macleod stood and looked at Ross for a moment, then nodded. This was Jona Nakamura. A mistake in getting pregnant? Jona was thorough, planned, on top of things. Jona was the person who'd taught Macleod how to stay balanced, how to get rid of any negative emotions, and now here she was possibly pregnant and not telling anyone.

'Maybe I should get Hope to speak to her.'

'No,' said Ross, 'maybe you should keep out of it until she tells you.' Then after a long pause, Ross added, 'sir.'

Ross was right. It actually wasn't Macleod's business and tomorrow was another day. He needed to get the work done and then get on with whatever else came his way. What bothered him was Jona's possible pregnancy seemed more of an issue to him than potentially four deaths on the ferries.

Chapter 08

Hope generally didn't spend that much time with Clarissa in the field as both held the rank of sergeant, although Hope was the superior within the team. Macleod generally split them, happy to let them work either alone or to take Ross or another constable with them. Ross, however, was going nowhere. Macleod had him checking through the passenger list for any random detail that could pull out a potential killer. He'd be cross-referencing, checking credit cards, all in a hopeful attempt at trying to narrow down who had been on all four ferries.

In the back of Hope's mind was the idea that maybe this one murder had been it, maybe the other, suicides, and then someone had taken advantage, but there were too many things that were out of line. All the suicides hadn't been seen. There was no confirmation that these people had jumped of their own accord. Were they really that upset that they were being driven to suicide? Macleod, of course, had been right. You'd find it all out in the details of the people. You needed to know who they were, what they did, what their lives were. She understood why they were investigating, why the Coastguard needed their assistance. This was the murder team's bread and butter, and Hope truly believed they'd get to the bottom of it.

One thing about being with Clarissa was that Hope wasn't driving. If she was with Macleod, she automatically took the wheel, and she agreed with Clarissa's view that Macleod drove like a pedestrian. Hope didn't think he drove that well either. She didn't know if it was an age thing or the fact the man was just a poor driver. But having gone now with Clarissa and sitting in the small green sports car, half of her was wondering if maybe she should go back with Macleod. Hope had forgotten her hair tie, and her red hair was streaking out the back as they raced along the motorway south.

Clarissa seemed to be in her element, a headscarf tied around her head, the top down on the vehicle, and Hope wondered if Clarissa would turn around and start waving at every car she overtook. To give her due credit, Clarissa was a very good driver, and she knew how to handle her own car. That, however, did not make up for the fact that Hope would rather have been in a normal hatchback or saloon with the heating on and not being required to drink so quickly because the cool air meant any beverage was cold in less than five minutes.

'Not long till we're into the Derbyshire Hills. You'll see how this thing handles then,' said Clarissa. Hope wrapped her arms around herself. She could do with her man here. Could John wrap her up? Hope normally wore a leather jacket, open. She liked that with something with colour underneath to highlight the black, but instead it was zipped up tight, her arms folded around her and tucked in under her armpits. Beside her, wrapped in her shawl, Clarissa looked radiant.

Soon the motorway faded, and the Derbyshire Hills were as Clarissa had predicted, filled with curved roads that Clarissa seemed to have a sixth sense about. The speed at which she took corners made Hope wonder if she could see round them in a fashion that no normal human could? She overtook people at speed, dropping the gears often to get that burst of power. When they eventually pulled up at a house halfway up a hill in an old mining village, Hope staggered out of the car and then feigned a number of stretches.

'Just tired sitting there so long,' she said.

'See? That was more fun than driving with Macleod, wasn't it? I still remember the old pursuit driving back in the day. They said I could handle the car, then of course, I went off into art and antiques. 'Wasted,' they said to me.'

'We're off back up towards Scotland after this,' said Hope. 'I think we might do well to find somewhere and stop for the night. If Macleod needs me quickly, I'll fly.'

Clarissa shot her a look, then marched up and rapped the front door of a small cottage. She watched the curtains at the side being pulled back and then the door opened to a woman that stood almost six feet, with wide shoulders and a thunderous look on her face.

'Yes?'

Charming, thought Hope, and reached inside her jacket to pull out her identification. 'Excuse me. I'm Detective Sergeant Hope McGrath. This is Detective Sergeant Clarissa Urquhart. We need to talk to Marie Culshaw regarding the death of her husband. Would you be her?'

'No. I'm Angela, Angela Sinclair. Marie is my sister, and I don't think you'll be able to speak to her.'

'Why is that?'

'She hasn't been well since he died. She's not coping.'

'I'm afraid this is part of a police investigation. I'd rather come in and talk socially with her, but if needs be, we can go down to the station. I don't wish it to go that far.'

'You'd haul a widow down to the station? It's barbaric. Is that what they do up in Scotland?'

'Up in Scotland, we do the same as they do down in England. There's been a murder, and we need to talk to Mrs Culshaw about the death of her husband. There may be possible links.'

'If you must, wait there,' said the woman firmly, and shut the door in their face.

'You want me to kick it in?' asked Clarissa. Hope nearly reacted, put her hands out to stop Clarissa doing it, before realising the woman was joking.

'Yes, it was a bit strong, wasn't it?' said Hope. 'You might have to—'

'You're getting like him. Do you know that?'

'What?' asked Hope.

'Macleod. You're just like Macleod. Oh, here we come. Here's the difficult person in front of who you want to talk to as a witness, and guess what? Let's get old Clarissa to take them to one side.'

'Well, you're damn good at it,' said Hope, not batting an eyelid.

'You just better hope our roles don't get reversed. I give you a pleasant drive down in the car and you dump me with this?'

'It's the joy of rank or, in fact, seniority. We have the same rank.'

The door opened and the intense face of Angela Sinclair looked back at them. 'She's in the living room but five minutes.'

Hope stepped forward and held her hand up. 'Mrs Sinclair, this is a police investigation. You're not a medical doctor. You don't have a patient that you think could be compromised by prolonged questioning. If they said to me five minutes, it would be five minutes. I will take what time I need with your sister. I'd kindly ask that you talk to my colleague.'

'Your colleague? Why would I want to talk to your colleague?'

'You probably don't. She wants to talk to you. We need to get a rounded view of Mr Culshaw.'

'Well, okay, but just once I see that Marie's all right.'

'Is it this way?' said Hope, marching into the hall and trying a door. She opened it to see a woman sitting on the sofa, looking up with sullen eyes. 'Excuse me. Are you Mrs Marie Culshaw?'

'That's me,' she said in a voice that was like a church whisper.

'I'm Detective Inspector Hope McGrath, and I need to speak to you about the death of your husband. It's just routine inquiry into a different murder investigation we've got.'

'Okay,' the woman said quietly, and sat back in the seat. Hope watched as her sister sat down beside her, right on the edge of the sofa, staring hard at Hope.

'I'd like to ask you first about your husband. What sort of a man was he?'

'Andrew? Andrew was hard to live with, but he had some good sides to him. He was a loving guy in a lot of ways. I remember when we got married, and he would—'

'He used to smack her about,' said Angela. ' I'd come in and I'd see her. She'd be red around the chops. He used to humiliate her at times, pulled down her trousers, and smack her like a child.'

'Is that right?' asked Hope. 'Is your sister correct in what she's saying?'

'Yes,' came the whisper.

'Well, I'm deeply sorry for that. Did he do anything else other than—'

'Oh, he did things, all right. I mean he was wicked. Wicked man.'

'Don't talk about him like that. You didn't understand us. You didn't.'

'"I didn't understand" my arse, Marie. We told you before he should have got it earlier. Best thing that happened to him.'

'Did you take that trip together, alone, away from the rest of the family?' asked Hope.

'We did. You see, we'd won tickets for the trip. That's why we were on it. Andrew was actually quite excited. He'd…, well, he'd packed certain things, things that would've—'

'He packed your dirty costumes. That's what he did.' Hope glanced over at Clarissa and gave her a nod.

'I'm afraid, Miss Sinclair, I need to speak to you. The sergeant will need to speak to your sister alone. If you'd come with me.'

'I'm staying here.'

Clarissa stood up and marched over, before positioning herself between Angela and her sister. 'If you're staying here, we'll have to do that bit down the station. Better if I speak to you now. Up, please.' Clarissa put an arm under the woman, lifted her up, and escorted her briskly out through the door.

'You can speak more freely now,' said Hope, 'now that your sister is gone. Just say things as they are. I won't be shocked. You'll be amazed at how much we see in our work. You were saying Andrew won the tickets?'

'He did. He won these tickets. Then he came home with some more outfits. He liked me to dress for him, that sort of thing. He was quite generous that way, but he did use to hit me, especially if I didn't like the outfit.' The woman was looking off to one side and Hope felt so sorry for her.

'Was he getting any help for that?' she asked.

'We had gone to several counselling sessions here, there, and everywhere. I was advised I should leave him, offered refuge, women's refuge and things, but I was never going to get rid of him. My husband, he'd told me he loved me. I couldn't walk away from him. Do you understand that?'

Hope wasn't really sure she did, but she said so anyway. 'When you went onto the ferry,' asked Hope, 'what happened?'

'Well, that's the thing. We had a bit of a row. Andrew was not happy.'

'Why was that?' asked Hope.

'I'd put the wrong top on, or rather I'd worn a top that he wanted a certain garment underneath, but frankly, it was a bit revealing, so I decided to say no. He hit me. Then when we were on board, he turned around and he told me that I looked like nothing good. He was the one who could make me look better. He was highly abusive. In that sense, it was a pity because he did love me.'

It sounded like a funny sort of love to Hope, but she decided to continue with the line of questioning. 'You had counselling sessions. Where was that?'

'We actually ended up in Glasgow for a lot of them. A Dr Stevens. He was recommended to us. Dr Stevens was good. She was helping him, but Andrew was a tough case. I'm not sure he appreciated having a female counsellor to begin with. I did though. I appreciated it. It felt safer with another woman there.'

'Did the sessions help?'

'In a way, they did. You see, she had Andrew doing nice things for me. He suddenly would stop hitting me. He'd suddenly make the dinner, or he'd take me out somewhere.

Then it would go wrong, he'd buy a dress, and really, you wouldn't wear these things out and about, but he'd insist on it and I'd get annoyed. He'd then get angry. He'd end up hitting me when we came home, especially if I hadn't worn what he wanted.'

'Dr Stevens, did she tell you to leave him at any point?'

'She did. She even gave a name of refuge and places. Andrew found them and went nuts, but I didn't choose to leave him. There was good inside him. All my sister can see is the bad side.'

From the hall outside, Hope could hear some swearing, swearing referring to a man in the vilest of terms.

'Yes, she does sound like she doesn't like him,' said Hope. 'When you rowed on the ferry, what happened then?'

'He stormed off, went upstairs. That's the last I saw of him. He threw himself off the top. I'd like to think the guilt got to him. Then I feel guilty about saying that. I didn't want him dead. Never wanted him dead. I wanted him to see, to be better. I wanted him to be a proper husband.'

'When you were on the boat, was there anyone close to you? Anyone you saw looking at you?'

'Whole boat stared at me when he started rowing and he hit me.'

'Did anyone interfere at that point, especially when he hit you?'

'Some men came over and that's when Andrew went upstairs.'

'Did any of them follow him?'

'Not as far as I could tell,' said Marie. Hope continued the questioning for another half an hour but learned nothing that she hadn't learned in those first engagements. As they left the house, Angela Sinclair saw them to the door. 'I'm so glad he got that ticket,' she said.

'Why?' asked Hope.

'Because that's what made him go up there. That's what made him jump. Go to his death. She's better off without him. She won't see that, but she is better off without him.'

'Are you sure he won the ticket?'

'Totally. He was too tight to buy something like that. The only thing he spent money on was stuff to make Marie look—well, look like you know what, tart, and a pretty dirty one at that.'

'We'll let you get back to looking after your sister,' said Hope. The door was slammed shut behind them. She sat down in the small green sports car, and Clarissa joined her.

'Guess it's back up the road,' she said, 'but it's interesting.'

'How come?' asked Clarissa.

'Warring couple. Everyone seems to be a warring couple in counselling.'

'Everyone except the fellow that fell off the boat in Leverburgh. His wife was already dead.'

'Maybe they were warring before that.'

'But they're all warring with each other. So what? We've got four random people just going around in boats looking for somebody who's having a fight and then bumping one of them off?'

'I know it sounds a bit wild at the moment,' said Hope. 'It's a feeling in the gut.'

'Seoras said that he had a feeling in his gut as well,' said Clarissa. 'I'm struggling to swallow that. We can't go on gut anyway. We need to find some evidence.'

'You don't think the sister could be a suspect?'

'If it was a one-off,' said Hope. 'I would. But four? Why kill off the other three? Practice?'

'You've come across practice before, I thought.'

Hope thought down to earlier times in her career when the Skye Bridge was blown up, the shooting at Fort Augustus along the line of Neptune's steps.

'This doesn't feel like that. It really doesn't.' Hope's head threw back against the headrest as Clarissa spun the car around and drove off back into the Derbyshire countryside. *Next time,* thought Hope. *Next time, I drive, even if I have to hire my own car to get here.*

Chapter 09

Ross started sifting through the statements from the passengers of the ferry. Occasionally, he would glance out of the window of Stornoway Police Station, but in truth, it wasn't the greatest view he'd ever seen. The station was tucked away a few streets behind the main Stornoway thoroughfare, if you could call it that, on a road that swept into town through Bayhead and followed the harbour round before finding its way out to the other side of town to one of the town's supermarkets. The day had clouded over and outside was cold.

Ross furtively looked up the street at the curry house on the corner, his stomach rumbling, knowing that it was lunchtime, but such a main meal was not on the cards. He looked at the reheated noodles in a plastic tub, and knew why he hadn't eaten many of them.

Standing up, he made his way out of the office. Scurrying along the corridor until he found a kitchen, Ross grabbed an apple he'd left there earlier, took it back to his office, and sat down again. He moved as if he was alone, but in truth, there were busy constables around him but to him, they could have been in a different world.

He was processing, churning through the statements he'd read. Every now and again, Ross would put another one in front of him, and his pen would shoot across to the blank piece of paper, a way of cross-referencing. He could do it on the computer, but Ross liked to see the old-fashioned pencil and pen, which seemed to connect more with him, despite how good he was on a computer.

His train of thought was broken as the door opened, and he heard a measured but firm set of footsteps coming towards him. He looked up knowing it would be the face of his boss.

'Sir?' said Ross.

'How are we getting on?'

'Well, Daphne Walsh doesn't seem to have been seen by anybody. I've gone through statements again, and the only person I can see who actually saw her before she went into the water was a child who was down on the lower deck at a window. They have these big round ones. I guess a small child can sit in them so the little girl was looking out watching for dolphins, and then she saw Daphne come past.'

'That must have been a shock for her. So, she raised the alarm then?'

'Indirectly. She paddled along and told her parents that she'd seen somebody go in. They didn't think much of it but thought they should report it, at which point, most of the crew went up on deck and could see Mrs Walsh out the back of the vessel in the water. They called the attention of the master, the boat turned around, Mayday given to the Coastguard. Everything ran from there, sir.'

'Did nobody see her up on deck?'

'No. Nobody near her. People saw her going up to go on deck, but nobody actually saw her up there.'

'What about people who went up at the same time as Daphne? People trying to go up the stairs, or disappearing out on deck?'

'Hard. You've got a couple of hundred people in this boat, and some of the steps you can go up without actually going out on deck as well. I'm not getting any consistent picture of someone around the same time as her. Most reports are very general descriptions; brown hair, maybe five feet seven, up to five feet eleven. There's nothing concrete you could pin on anyone.'

'So, what you're telling me is, Ross, that we have all these people on this ferry, and nobody manages to spot her going upstairs, and then going into the water?'

'Oh, they spotted her going up the stairs,' said Ross, 'there's just nothing after that.'

'I don't believe that for a minute.'

'It gets tricky though, sir, because she didn't go up the stairs once, she went up several times. Trying to weed out who actually saw her on the last occasion, I've also tried to see if anybody was following her up on each occasion, but there's no pattern. Although to be truthful, I'm not sure half of these people would have noticed.'

'Somebody must have.'

'Why?' asked Ross. 'Why would you? People won't recall that. They won't recall who's gone up. Some of them are struggling to recall even seeing her. Several of the people I've interviewed said they saw this person going up, and then I showed a photograph of who it was, and they said, 'Well, that's not the one I was talking about.''

'Come on, Ross. There must be something. This is number four. We know they're being killed.'

'We know one's been killed, sir. One was murdered and that's Daphne Walsh. The others, we don't know, do we?'

'Yes, yes, Ross. I know what you're saying, but four passengers overboard this close together, blast it, why? Why? What is it with this? Anyway, Ross, I need to go and speak to Mr Walsh. He's downstairs. Not going to be the most pleasant of my duties.'

'Would you like me to sit in on it, sir?' asked Ross.

'No, it's fine. I'll take it. To be truthful, I'm not sure how much we're going to learn. It's going to be a background search. Nothing more, nothing less. Nobody puts him anywhere near once she's gone up on deck, do they?'

'No,' said Ross.

'Well, in that case, you need to find the connection. You need to find out why these people have been killed. What's the key to it? I'll speak to you later.'

'Oh, sir,' said Ross, 'I was thinking, dinner tonight? Maybe we should get one a bit earlier, around teatime.'

'Well, I haven't really thought about it, Ross. I don't know where we're going to be going.'

'There's that curry house up in the corner. We've been there before, remember?'

'As I recall last time, Clarissa had me up trying to sing. I hope you're not looking for a repeat performance.'

'No, sir. Except for the biryani.'

Macleod allowed Ross a half-smile, more for encouragement than actually feeling any particular humour about what Ross has said. Macleod was too involved at the moment, his mind racing through possibilities. He never settled while the case was on, always thinking.

Ross was different. Ross could snap into a mode and snap

out. When a case was happening, it consumed Macleod. Jane
had told him so, told him to go and get things done before
coming back. She said she lost her partner every time a case
kicked off, and he struggled to correct her on that.

Macleod walked out of the office and down the stairs
towards the interview room. He knocked on the door, and a
constable let him in. A man was sitting behind a desk, a cup of
tea in front of him, and he was hunched over. He had black
hair, clearly uncombed, and a shirt that looked ruffled.

'Mr Walsh, it's me Detective Inspector Macleod. Again, can
I offer you my condolences on the loss of your wife?'

The man slowly raised his head and Macleod could see the
red eyes.

'Thank you, Inspector,' he said, and then put his head down.

'I'll try and be as quick as I can,' said Macleod, 'but we think
that your wife's demise may have been one of many and I need
to look into her background.'

'One of many?' asked the man suddenly, lifting his face to
Macleod. 'Why would Daphne be one of many? What . . .?'

'I regret to inform you, sir, that your wife was injected with
a substance that would've paralyzed her, and we believed she
was thrown off the ferry.'

'Daphne? Why? I mean, what did Daphne ever do to
anyone?'

'Well, most people can offend someone,' said Macleod. 'I
know that the two of you were rowing before she went
upstairs.'

'You don't think I did it, do you?' said the man suddenly. 'I
wouldn't touch her. I wouldn't . . . , I mean, yes, we'd argue,
but I wouldn't . . . , I wouldn't do anything to Daphne.'

'I don't believe that you did, sir. I certainly don't believe that you were up on deck and in any way, were responsible for your wife's demise. I just bring it up to try and find out a bit of background about Mrs Walsh.'

'About Daphne; she's called Daphne,' said the man.

Macleod could feel a resentment when he said 'Mrs Walsh', something much stronger than he would've thought of. He didn't read it that the man was insisting on the woman's first name because she was somehow precious but rather as a reaction to something else. It may have seemed cruel, but Macleod thought he should press on with the point.

'Daphne, Mrs Walsh, was arguing with you about something. What was that about?'

'Daphne argued about a lot of things. An awful lot of things.'

'Such as?'

'Daphne had a problem. She never saw things anybody else's way; she could get fiery, violent.'

'Did she ever hit you?'

'Yes. Often, frequently, but we were trying to work it. We went to see a counsellor, Dr Jacobs. Although she seemed to get worse then, in a lot of ways. She didn't like to go.'

'And he called her Mrs Walsh, didn't he?'

The man's teeth clenched. 'Yes,' he snarled. 'Mrs Walsh, she hated Mrs Walsh, she was Daphne. Even Daphne Walsh would've done, but he kept calling her Mrs Walsh.'

'Why did she get upset by that?' asked Macleod, 'it seems fairly normal, a detachment, maybe, from a counsellor to his client.'

'It was her thing, Inspector. You need to understand that about Daphne. If Daphne saw something as black and white and you saw it different, Daphne was right. Daphne was always right in Daphne's mind and if people didn't change, she got angry. I think Dr Jacobs wanted to try and get that anger out to then try and control it, but it didn't work. I didn't get what he was doing.'

'How long were you with Dr Jacobs?'

'We were still seeing him. We went over to Aberdeen as he was recommended to us by some friends of ours. I don't have a particular problem with him, except that, well, it didn't work, did it? She got angry. Maybe that's what happened, maybe that's why they threw her off.'

'No, I'm afraid not, Mr Walsh. Your wife was murdered. She was injected, as I said, with a substance that paralyzed her, and then she was thrown off the ferry. I need to know if there's anybody who had cause to hate her.'

'Cause to hate, yes. Daphne upset people. She was challenged in that way. Like I said, she couldn't see how somebody else could be right and she could be wrong and if it became a bone of contention, she would lit; she would go after them.'

'Had she ever hit anybody else?'

'Once, but I had to stop her several times.'

'Did you ever think you got anywhere with the counselling?' ask Macleod.

'We did at one point. We were going to move and take up a new home, out in the country; it would've been good for her, but then she ruined all that. She attacked the guy who was selling the house to us. This is the thing; anytime you made plans with Daphne, anytime you sorted something out, suddenly something would go wrong. She'd get angry, she'd get violent. It was a full-time job just trying to control that. Do you understand me, inspector?'

Macleod looked into eyes that were now streaming with tears. 'I tried hard. I tried damn hard. You can't do more as a husband, and every time, she wrecked it. Every time, that thing inside of her, that bloody, arrogant, son-of-a-bitch, festering ego wrecked it.' The man put his hand up to his chin, which was suddenly trembling. Macleod could see him physically shake.

'When she couldn't hit other people, she hit you, didn't she?'

'Yes, she did. Then she'd tell me, 'Why the hell am I Mrs Walsh? I'm not Mrs Walsh anymore,' and she'd hit me with whatever, anything at hand. On the ferry, she had a go at me because I told her that I had made another appointment for Dr Jacobs. She went up on deck because she couldn't find anything to hit me with, to attack me. With the way she was, I thought she was best left alone.'

Macleod sat back as the man began to cry again. He watched the shoulders shudder, the sobs now coming hard and heavy. As Macleod leaned back in the seat, he wondered just what the connection was between all of these people.

'One last thing, Mr Walsh. Why were you making this trip?'

'Because we won it,' he said, 'we won the trip. A couple of pairs of tickets arrived. Daphne apparently had won it, and these tickets came addressed to me. I thought it was strange, but they gave us the tickets after Daphne contacted them, so we went. That was a bone of contention too. She kept telling me she had never entered anything. It would be like her though, put it in my name and if we didn't win, she could blame me.'

'But you think she did actually enter something?'

'Well, what other explanation is there?' said the man, his eyes still streaming.

'I give my condolences,' said Macleod standing up. 'Thank you for coming in to speak. The constables will assist you in any way they can.'

Macleod left the room and picked up a telephone in a nearby office. He called direct to the ferry company asking what competitions they'd run when they were giving away tickets, and they told him none in the last year. He put the phone down carefully. Maybe that was something to look at.

Chapter 10

Derbyshire had been hills and swinging roads where Hope had hung on as the nippy green car of Clarissa Urquhart had sped along. Now they were up in the Lake District with vast views of water and quaint towns, one of which they'd stopped in for cake and coffee before driving to the home of Gerald Lyndhurst. The man was in his garden on a rather dour day, down on his knees attending to what Hope could only describe as yellow flowers. She'd been a city girl all her life and botany was something that had never interested her.

Clarissa Urquhart parked the car and she saw the man raise his head briefly before putting it back down again, focusing on the foliage before him. Hope walked along to the man's gate, thought twice about entering and shouted across, 'Excuse me, are you Gerald Lyndhurst?'

The man stood up and Hope could see pads on his knees. He must have been gardening for quite some time.

'Yes, that's me. Who are you?'

'My name's Detective Sergeant Hope McGrath from Inverness police station. This is Detective Sergeant Clarissa Urquhart. Do you mind if we have a word, sir?'

'Scottish police. This'll be about Peter, isn't it?'

Hope could see the man begin to shake slightly, but he tried to hold his bearing.

'It's probably better if we go inside. I'm just about finished here anyway. You couldn't give me a hand, could you? There's a couple of tools there in that,' he said pointing to a bucket, 'just to bring into the house. Don't like to leave them out in case I forget. They get rusty you see. Rusty tools don't help in the garden. I always like things nice and neat. Peter was the same.'

The man didn't wait, but slowly trudged off towards his front door and Hope picked up the tools. She saw Clarissa entering the garden, so the pair then walked towards the front door of a small cottage. The garden around them was immaculate. Hope wondered how somebody could keep it so well. As she stepped inside the front door, she heard a shout from the kitchen.

'I hope you don't mind, but we don't wear shoes in this house.'

Hope caught Clarissa's look of, 'The man's a nutter,' but considering his friend had just died, Hope acquiesced to the man's request, slipping off her boots before walking into the kitchen behind him.

'Would you like a cup of tea, because if you don't mind, I'm going to have one. I was trying not to think about him today, trying to just do. You've kind of screwed that up.'

'I'm sorry, but we have to investigate.'

'Investigate,' said the man suddenly. 'Why? He fell off the ferry.'

'He certainly came off the ferry,' said Hope. 'I am afraid that whether that happened as an accident or not is very much up for debate.'

Hope saw the man almost stumble and she reached out,

getting a hand under his arm and steadying him.

'Maybe I should take you through. Sergeant Urquhart, maybe you could finish the tea.'

Hope assisted the man over to a door, to what she presumed would be the front lounge. As they reached the door, the man stopped suddenly. 'No more than five minutes,' he said.

'What?' asked Clarissa.

'The tea. No more than five minutes. Milk second.' Clarissa's face was in total bemusement but Hope quickly nodded at her to just get on with what she was doing. The red-haired Sergeant assisted the man in to the sofa inside.

The living room was immaculate as well, everything in its place, a set of antimacassars on the back of the sofa, and around the walls were neatly framed pictures. Hope noticed that a few of them were wrong. The frames that were up against the wall were too small. Sun clearly streamed in through the front window and the wood panelling on the wall had faded around where the photograph had been. They'd clearly been replaced with a smaller photograph and the wood that was not exposed was a different colour than that which had been exposed the whole time.

'Can I get you anything else, Mr. Lyndhurst?'

'No, no, please just sit.' Hope sat beside the man and he placed his hand into hers. 'It's been difficult,' he said. 'Really difficult.'

'Well, it's hard to lose friends,' said Hope.

'He wasn't a friend. You have to understand that, my dear. We've kept this going for years. He was everything to me; you get that? Everything, but he wouldn't tell anyone. He wouldn't tell anyone because of me. I wanted it all quiet.'

'Are you telling me that the two of you were intimate?' asked

Hope.

'I guess we were in that sense a little, although we were very platonic. I mean, look at me, look at the age I am. This wasn't some sort of hot affair or anything. We just were easy in each other's company, really easy. I guess it developed out of that.'

'Nothing wrong with that though, is there?'

'You tell that to people around here.' said the man suddenly. 'There's always someone, isn't there? Always someone that doesn't like it. The way you are.'

'Have you suffered before?'

'Yes,' said Gerald. 'I lost a partner twenty years ago.'

'This is the second partner that's died on you?'

'No. The first one didn't die. I lost him. He was hounded out. We were both hounded out and then he couldn't take it.'

'Hounded by who?'

'Those who don't like men with men. This time I kept it quiet. I said to Peter we keep quiet. We'd just have ourselves, but Peter wanted…, he wanted to come out. He wanted to tell everyone.'

Hope looked up at the wall again, and noticed that many photographs contained an image of Peter Hughes. All the photographs, all the frames that looked out of place, they had Peter in them.

'You didn't have his photo on the wall, did you?' asked Hope. 'I see you do now.'

'Guilt,' said Gerald. 'That's why they're up there. It's guilt.'

'How much pressure did he put on you to open up to everyone else about your relationship?'

'He was determined to do it. I loved him but he really was forceful about it. Constantly at me. I couldn't take it. I couldn't take it. I thought, well, if we can get help, if we know how to do this. He wanted me to go to one of his counsellors, one of the ones that just…, they want everything out in the open. I said no. I said, "We go to somebody who's there just to help us both. Not somebody of any particular sides.'"

'How did that work out?' asked Hope.

'We went to a Dr Greene in Inverness, one of these relationship counsellors. We looked him up. He seemed quite good, but we still struggled. Peter never changed his mind. He wanted to force, he wanted to push the issue, so we argued at times. Dr Greene said Peter was the issue. He had this obsession with wanting to be out in public, wanting to flaunt, he said. Flaunt things. Not just to have things the way they are, but to flaunt them. It's almost like he wanted the issue out there. He thrived on the issue being out there. I didn't. I just wanted the quiet life and him.'

'Who told you about Dr Greene?' asked Hope.

'I just looked him up. We liked Inverness. We couldn't go around here. We couldn't go local, and we'd made several trips up to Inverness already. There's a little haunt up there; maybe you'll know it. There's a little cottage, just beyond Beauly but it meant we could go and see Dr Greene without worrying about anybody else, knowing the man was discreet. To be fair to him, I don't believe he ever told anyone down here about what we were coming to him for.'

'What were you doing on the ferry?' asked Hope. 'Wasn't that a little bit overt, going together?'

'Yes. When we went to Inverness, we travelled apart, but Peter was always wanting us to travel together. I thought, well, if we take a trip, we can travel together. We don't have to show people that we're a couple. We can just be two friends. That worked for me.'

'You planned a trip?' asked Hope.

Before the man could answer, Clarissa came through with some tea. She placed a cup down in front of Gerald and Hope saw the man's face.

'Nice and wet that one, love. Get that down you. Help you a bit.' Hope saw that Clarissa's comment about the tea was not well received.

'I just don't feel like it at the moment,' said Peter, pushing the cup to one side.

'You were telling me about the trip,' said Hope as Clarissa sat down on a couch opposite.

'Well, the trip came about because Peter won it. He won some tickets in the post. He said to me, 'Have you ever been on this ferry over to Mull?' I said no, and the next thing Peter had booked some accommodation. It was a bed and breakfast. He booked a double room for us, a proper double bed. I said no, got him to change it and we took a little cottage instead. That was him, always forcing the issue. "Let's go in there and just show everybody who we are." Some of us don't want that. I'd done it last time. You don't understand the things that they say. Are either of you?'

'No,' said Clarissa, and then she started as Hope announced, 'Yes. I'm bi.'

'You see that's what I don't want.' He pointed at Clarissa. 'You haven't said anything even nasty, but you reacted with shock and it puts a barrier up. The last time it was worse than that. Threats, violence. You have to be so careful.'

'I can understand that from your experience,' said Hope. 'But back to the tickets. You said he won them?'

'Yes, they came through the post. He said he couldn't remember entering anything but clearly, he had. Peter was a bit sketchy like that. I was the ordered one. I was the one who would plan things meticulously. A pair of tickets arrived, and he said to go and use them. Then he just goes on, wildly books a B&B for the pair of us with a double room. We sorted that out. I like a bit of control on things. Do you understand that? Is that a bad thing?'

'No, it isn't,' said Hope. 'Tell me about the trip then, because you were arguing.'

'Well,' said Gerald, 'Peter had booked this double room and then I changed it. We were on the ferry and Peter came back again and again at me saying we need to start showing who we are; we need to live our real lives. We had spoken before in front of Dr Greene. I couldn't, from what happened before, I couldn't do it. It put a massive strain on our relationship because he kept forcing things. He kept saying we should do this. Do this, do that. For me, it was becoming too much. That's why we rowed. He disappeared off.'

Hope sat back watching the man stare and she could see he had disappeared into another mind. They stayed for another ten minutes asking similar questions, but it was clear the man did not know much. As they returned to Clarissa's car, Hope was aware of her staring at her.

'What's up?' asked Hope.

'You kept that quiet,' said Clarissa.

'Kept what quiet?'

'Bi. I wouldn't have put you down for that.'

'Why?' asked Hope.

'Look at you. Six-foot, red hair, turn all the guys' heads. You wouldn't need a woman.'

'It's not about need,' said Hope, 'and, like Gerald, I don't advertise. I don't keep it a secret either, though. That man's living in fear. Living in fear of something that happened to him a long time ago.'

'But he was also living with friction,' said Clarissa. 'Did you notice that? And he's been off to a counsellor. Things are beginning to line up.'

'They are, aren't they?' said Hope. 'You should talk to Seoras. See what he knows about his victim.'

Chapter 11

Ross shovelled a pile of rice and lamb tikka up to his mouth before washing it down with a swig of Coke. He would have enjoyed having a beer with his dinner, but he was still working, and had wandered along to the curry house despite the fact that Macleod had not joined him. He had been told by the Inspector he'd be there at six o'clock, but six had made it to a quarter past and Ross had ordered. Now at a quarter to seven, he was almost finished his meal, and there had still been no sign of the Inspector. Ross found it hard to do things on his own at times like these. He and the Inspector were coming into a different station, although they'd been there several times now.

Still, he felt that as a team they should be sticking together, to eat, to work. Macleod's dedication—or was it obsession?—with work made it hard for Ross to apply mealtimes in a sensible fashion, but if he had waited for Macleod, who knows when he would have eaten, maybe even not at all, and at midnight, the curry house wouldn't have been open. Ross wasn't one for a kebab, so he made sure he got to eat what he wanted.

As his plate was being cleared away, Ross saw a constable

appear at the door of the curry house and then approach the table.

'Inspector Macleod would like you back at the station soon as, Constable.'

'Thank you,' said Ross, and immediately stood up before wiping his mouth with his napkin. He paid quickly and took the short walk down the street into the police station to find Macleod sitting in front of his laptop.

'Ross, can you get this thing set up?'

'For what, sir?'

'The team, we need the team, we need to talk to the team. It's not doing it. I don't know why it's not doing it. I pressed the buttons, the ones you said last time and it's not doing it.'

'Yes, sir. On it now,' said Ross. Thirty seconds later the screen was showing a picture of Clarissa which was shortly joined by a picture of Jona. Ross said nothing more, but Macleod kept staring over at him.

'You can say it, you can say it.'

'Say what, sir?'

'The old man is an idiot. What did I do wrong?'

Ross didn't know quite how to play this. The real question was, what did he do right because he hadn't done anything correctly. Ross was trying to work out how something that should have been fairly simple was not executed correctly by a man who obviously had intelligence.

'I'll take you through it another time, sir; probably best we should crack on.' Macleod gave him a stare and Ross knew that Macleod understood what the comment really meant.

'Is McGrath with you?' asked Macleod.

'She is here,' said Clarissa, and moved the laptop slightly. Macleod could see in the background Hope bringing over a couple of coffees.

'You're the one who wanted it, Hope. What have you found out?'

'We found a couple of similarities between our couples.'

'Couples?' queried Macleod.

'Yes, couples,' said Hope, 'I was down at Uist, which you know about, learning about Fred Martin. Now his wife had committed suicide before him, but they were both in counselling. He also won a trip to go on that ferry. We then went to Derbyshire where Marie Culshaw confirms that Andrew Culshaw and she were both in counselling, because of Andrew's abusive nature. She also said that they were on a trip that Andrew had won. We then went down to see Gerald Lyndhurst. Gerald was in a relationship with Peter Hughes. It was quiet and kept under the counter, but Peter wanted it brought out to the public. It was a cause of much distress amongst the pair and they went into counselling for it. This didn't seem to work for them either. Oh, and Peter also won a ticket on the ferry.'

'So did the Walshes,' said Macleod. 'They were in counselling as well. The coincidences just seem to be piling up here.'

'Thing is,' said Hope, 'they all have relationship issues, and I could easily look at this and say they all committed suicide when nobody saw them. They all disappeared off the ferry. If Jona hadn't brought up the fact that one of them had been injected with ketamine, might have probably opened and closed this quickly.'

'It's probably all we could have done,' said Macleod. 'Unlucky coincidence, but it doesn't sit right.'

'No,' said Hope, 'It could be that lemming effect. People see it, read it, do it. They all would have had a case for ending.'

'But we have Jona's belief that Daphne Walsh was murdered. You still have that belief, Jona?'

'Absolutely, Seoras. The thing is that she was injected with ketamine and was paralyzed. You don't do that to yourself. You certainly don't do that yourself and manage to get up and off a ferry. If you were going to kill yourself, you wouldn't go to that trouble, just throw yourself into the water. Throw yourself into the water, don't struggle, you'll soon sink.

'We've got people who won a ticket to get on a ferry. Our killer knows where they're going so they either work at the ferry company or they've sent the tickets. How's that working?' said Macleod. 'The ferry tickets that you get, they're interchangeable, you could phone up and change them anyway even if they arrived as a ticket. If you take a car, you have to put the car on.'

'Do we know anybody alive that actually got the ticket, or is it the person that always died? Just a moment,' said Macleod, 'We've still got Mr Walsh downstairs. He's in with one of the bereavement constables being looked after. Let me see if I can clarify this.' Macleod stood up and departed, leaving the rest of the team looking at each other.

'You eaten yet, Alan?' asked Hope to Ross.

'I have, I just went and did it. He had to pull me back.'

'Where did you go?' asked Clarissa.

'That Indian up in the corner from here.'

'The one where I had him singing in last time?'

'That's it,' said Ross.

'How far did you get through your meal before he grabbed you?'

'Just finished. He might not even have asked for me except he couldn't work the computer to get on the screen.'

'Write it down for him next time.'

'I don't need to write it down for him,' said Ross. 'It's just the fact that he gets worked up. He's not thinking about what he's doing. He's thinking about the case all the time, the way he gets, obsessed in it. Anyway, I wasn't going to wait for him this time for the food.'

'Well, that's an improvement,' said Hope. 'Sometimes you've got to manage your boss as well.'

Ross could hear the door behind him.

'Sometimes you just have to get a hold of him, Alan. You've got to be the one that moves him about. He's got to bend to you sometimes.'

Macleod appeared on the screen from the side. 'Who's Ross managing now?'

'Sorry, sir. Just a bit of chat,' said Clarissa. 'He's got many problems getting his car sorted.'

'He never told me,' said Macleod. 'Anyway, it's not what we're here to talk about. I've just been down to Mr Walsh. Apparently, there was a phone number to call and arrange. He thought it was quite funny because it seemed to be a mobile number. Here's the number, Ross. You need to get onto that.'

'If it's a mobile number, it's probably going to be a Pay-As-You-Go SIM,' said Ross. 'That's what I would do. That way you can't trace it. It might still be active, though I doubt it. Besides, they might have given a different number to each one. Soon as they've made the call, close it off. Then they can book the tickets for them.'

'Then we need to check where they were being booked from,' said Macleod. 'This is right up your alley, Ross. Get on this one, find out where those tickets were booked, how they were booked. Check the phone number. Let's get onto the other victims' families, check with them. See if they know how the tickets were bought, and how they were sent in.'

'The other commonality here,' said Hope, 'are the doctors.'

'Absolutely,' said Macleod. 'Where are the two of you at the moment?'

'In the Lake District, Seoras. Why?'

'Get back up to Scotland. Find those doctors, get their addresses, hunt them down and find out what was happening with these couples.'

'They were all seeking counselling. What's that got to do with it?' asked Clarissa.

'If they're all seeking counselling, and if it is a common trait,' said Macleod, 'somebody's got to know they were in counselling. Somebody's got to know these doctors. Somebody's got to know these records. You need to have a look and see if there's an angle through there.'

'It's pretty wide-ranging though, isn't it?' said Clarissa.

'Yes, it is. We haven't got a lot,' said Macleod. 'Except we've got four dead people with a few similarities. These similarities will bring us to who actually is carrying out these murders. Where are you off to first then?'

'Furthest south is Glasgow. I think it's a Dr Stevens,' said Hope. 'We'll head up and see Dr Stevens. Should be up there early afternoon. I'll try and contact the rest to see where they are. We've got Aberdeen and Inverness. I just need to make sure they're there.'

'Good,' said Macleod. 'Ross is going to tidy the ticket issue up. Jona, you're kind of redundant at the moment. Probably best if you head back to the station in Inverness, in case you're needed for elsewhere. Get some rest.'

'Will do, Inspector,' said Jona, glaring suspiciously at

Macleod. 'Only a phone call away if you need me.'

'What are you going to do, Seoras?' asked Hope.

'Think on it. I'm going to get some dinner as well. Was hungry earlier, but Ross didn't invite me along.'

Clarissa near spat when she saw Ross's face on the screen. With the screens closed down, Ross stood up and made his way over to a small desk he was operating out of. Then he watched Macleod slowly wander over to him.

'What did I do wrong in setting it up?'

'You know what to do. I've told you before. It's just you don't focus at times like this, sir, with respect.'

'What do you mean I don't focus?'

'You've got everything else going on in your head. It's like the technology doesn't work when it comes to times like this because you're not focused on the technology. You're focused on doing everything else. It's okay. I'm here.'

'Sorry for disturbing your food,' said Macleod. 'I think I might go and get some myself now. Let me know if you come up with anything.' Ross watched as the Inspector left the room and then gave his head a shake. As per usual, he'd been given the task of digging up and hunting out all the information. He called up Minchlines and asked them to check through where the tickets had been bought for the four couples.

As he held the line, he pondered how else to reach into the family background? He could check through medical records because they were all there for counselling. Maybe he needed to get a better idea of what for. Of course, it would be the deceased person's records he'd go for. It took ten minutes before Minchlines came back. The representative told Ross that all had been bought at different ferry points, had been paid for in cash, and had simply been booked in the names of those who got on board.

Ross asked for the names of those who were working, and it took the rest of the afternoon before Minchlines came back with the four workers who had sold the tickets. He spent his evening trying to trace them and to speak to them, only to find out that most of them hadn't got a clue who had paid. In truth, that wasn't surprising. They saw so many customers per day. There wasn't anything unusual about the bookings either. When Macleod came to see Ross at ten o'clock that night, Ross was feeling maxed out.

'Ross, go to the hotel. Go and get some sleep and go back at it tomorrow morning,' said Macleod.

'I've still got a lot to get through.'

'You can't talk to the families at this time of night. I'm telling you, you need to wind down, relax for the night.'

'Yes, sir,' said Ross, and he found himself walking back to the hotel. It was only when he got there and entered his room, he suddenly thought that the Inspector hadn't come with him. Then it dawned on Ross. When the sergeants had talked about Ross managing Macleod, he'd sworn that the man hadn't understood that it was him they were talking about. Macleod managing Ross. He'd heard. He'd flipping heard.

Chapter 12

J enny Trimble smiled, handed over the coffee, and took a step back from the counter, watching the customer disappear out the door. Two minutes left and then she was on her break. She'd get an hour off, an hour to herself. They'd left Islay when she was on shift and now as they crossed the waters over to the mainland, she would be able to step out on deck and take a cigarette in the sea air. She perfectly understood the clash of context, but like most things in life, Jenny didn't care.

She took a look at the ring on her finger and quietly slipped it off, putting it in her pocket. She generally wore it only when the captain would be about or the senior customer officer. Whenever she was fraternising with the rest of the crew, Jenny was more than happy to drop off the ring that spoke of her marriage. Who knew, on the way out to the upper deck, she might even, well, bump into one of the guys? She quickly thought through who was off at that time. You had to be careful though; it was obviously frowned upon, that sort of thing. It was much easier to do that onshore than it was on the vessel. There were always prying eyes somewhere.

Jenny looked up as Ken MacNeil walked in.

'Coffee, Jenny love.'

Ken was in his late thirties, but Jenny thought he managed to maintain a rather impressive figure. Yes, she was ten years his younger, but maybe that would help in her attempt to seduce Ken. He was a family man; she had heard that, but she wondered just how committed he was to his partner. You could always test them, always see. She had thought that he looked at her at times. He certainly gave her a smile every now and again, but she thought she recognised the eyes behind the smile. Was there a hunger for something?

'Just about to go off, Ken. What about yourself?'

'No, I'm just in, I'm going to be serving crew in about five minutes. You can come through there if you want and talk to me.'

It wasn't what Jenny was looking for. She didn't want to talk. 'Oh, it's fine, Ken,' she said, 'I think I might go up on the deck, take a bit of the fresh air, you know? I'm very hot here, there's all these lights.' She moved her hand just inside her blouse, adjusting her strap, making sure she was facing Ken when she did it. The man, however, was looking across at a packet of crisps. *Well, that was wasted*, she thought. *Totally wasted.*

She turned, took a cup, put it under the machine, pressed the button and waited for Ken's coffee to be dispensed.

'So, what's new, Ken? Everything all right at home?'

'Fine, the usual, kids out and about doing whatever, running us ragged, but yes, we're fine. What about you?'

'I was thinking to head off, but I've got to go and do one of these counselling sessions. Robbie wants it.'

'Really?' said Ken, now taking a bit more notice. 'Why is that then? You two okay?'

'We have never been okay, Ken. Robbie just thinks everything can be fixed. I mean, when your wife disappears out to here and does this sort of job, what do you expect?'

'Well, I'm sorry to hear that,' said Ken.

'I bet your wife doesn't complain like that, does she? How many kids is it now?'

'Six. Why do you think I'm working here?'

'Oh, you get to be clear of them for a couple of weeks.'

'No, I need the money. I'd rather be at home working, but I can't get the work at the moment, so you got to do what you got to do, haven't you? Why on earth are you here though, Jen? I don't understand it. Even if things aren't going that well between you and Robbie.'

'Well, sometimes you need a bit of space, don't you? Got to look around the field again.' The coffee machine finished and Jenny took the cup, put a lid on it and passed it through the small hatch to Ken.

'Cheers for that, Jenny. Well, I hope things get better for you. You know?'

'Ken, if you ever get a bit lonely out here, you know I'm available.'

'For what?' said Ken. 'You mean like a chat?'

How gullible was this guy? How stupid.

Jenny slid round the edge to the counter, came up towards Ken and put her hand into one of his. 'Now, if you really need something,' Jenny felt the hand being whipped away.

'Well, it's kind of you,' said Ken, 'but, no that's not me, but thank you, for the coffee,' he said, picking it up and striding out of the coffee cabin.

Jenny gave a sigh, she'd have to make do with one of the others. She had grown to like Ken; he had a good sense of humour and he obviously had plenty of kids, which seemed to make him more attractive, although Jenny didn't know why. She didn't want any of her own. Robbie was always pestering her at the start about kids; now he just pestered her about where she went some evenings. Well, if he was what he should be, it wouldn't be a problem—she'd be right there.

She watched Alice come in, an older member of staff. Alice simply gave her a nod, slid behind the counter and asked was there anything that she needed to know. Jenny shook her head, walked out of the coffee cabin, and went through a crew door that allowed her to step up inside the ship and move out to an outside deck.

She grabbed a cigarette, stuck it between her teeth, and lit it.

She heard somebody clanking up the steps. Jenny turned around to see no one there. Had they stopped? She turned away again and heard the clanking resume. She had been aware since they'd left of someone watching the cabin as she served her teas and coffees. They were hidden under a hat, and she hadn't been quite able to make out who they were or what they were doing. Still, it wasn't unusual. She got checked out by quite a number of people.

Jenny was fortunate in that sense; she had inherited a heck of a figure from her mother, one she hadn't ruined yet with childbirth. If people wanted to look at her, well, that was all right. She would rather they'd have come up and said something; she could gauge if there was any use for them but if they didn't, she couldn't very well just parade out there and ask them the question.

Jenny heard the clanking again, and this time she turned to see a large hat arriving towards the top of the stairs. She turned away, puffing on her cigarette, looking out to sea.

This was crap. She was stuck working on a boat, looking

to get what she could from a load of guys who quite frankly, either were married off or working two weeks at a time on their own. She needed to do something about this, go and work somewhere else, work away, maybe down in London or Glasgow or somewhere.

She heard footsteps moving around behind her on the open deck but that was the only sound. Yes, Jenny would have to sort her life out, get what she wanted.

A hand went over Jenny's mouth and suddenly a pain went into her shoulder. Somebody had just stuck a needle in her. The person held her tight, and Jenny felt her muscles beginning to relax. Soon she could hear everything, see everything, but she couldn't move. She would shake with terror except she couldn't.

Jenny toppled forward, her shoulder hitting the rail of the vessel. What had gone wrong with her? What was this person doing? She then realised her feet were being lifted up, her shoulder tipping over the rail, and her head began to point down towards the sea below. She saw the water breaking, the white waves spreading away from the boat and then she began to fall.

* * *

Ken took his drink with him and sat down in a seat in the crew quarters, sipping it, awaiting his time to go on shift. Jenny had been at it again. She had a heck of a figure, that was true, and a part of Ken liked her, but he also would like her to be a far nicer person. She was clearly doing the dirty on Robbie and the poor guy was trying to fight for her when really, he should just let her go. *Must be hard for him though*, he thought, *to have a catch like that. A woman who on the outside looked like everything a lot of men dream of, but on the inside, she was toxic. What on earth was she doing coming after Ken? He was married with six kids. There was no way he was ever going to leave, and that whole thing with her hand inside her blouse.*

Ken did not like being come on to. He never had his whole life. Ken sipped on his coffee, looked at his watch, and knew he was going to stand up again in two minutes and start taking over the shift. He looked out the window to his left, saw the sea, as ever, churning along, a sea he knew so well. The colour didn't change often, it was more the way the light shone on top of it. Some days were miraculous. He saw dolphins jumping alongside the boat, he saw the waves roll up high, but other days were calm. In truth, calmer days were better. He'd had this fill of wiping up other people's puke as they couldn't handle the vessel's motion.

For Ken, the motion had never been a problem. In fact, he remembered the first time Jenny had made a move towards him was when she'd been sick. She hadn't long been on the vessel, and they got a particularly rough day. She'd come through towards his quarters and been sick in the corridor outside. Ken had helped clean it up and get her to her bed. He remembered quite clearly how she'd stripped off and climbed inside. At the time he thought it was shocking, but maybe it was just the more modern ways of people, ones that he didn't understand. When she threw back the blanket and invited him in, he understood perfectly what she wanted and that was when he left.

Dear Jenny, he thought, *she could be such a person. It's such a shame.* He hated to see someone throwing their life away like that.

Something went past the window outside. It was brief, but it was definitely large, maybe person-sized.

'Someone's just gone in, 'said Ken loudly in the crew room. 'Someone's gone in.'

'Well, run outside and have a look, see what it is, Ken,' said the second officer, and Ken stepped out from his fixed table, made a run through corridors up onto the upper outside deck. By the time he got there and looked out, he could see a figure in the sea.

'Overboard!' he shouted. 'Man overboard!' Behind him came the footsteps of the second officer.

'What do you mean, Ken?' the man shouted.

'Man overboard in the sea. I can see. I can see from here.'

'Keep your eyes on,' said the second officer and ran off, presumably to tell the master of the vessel, or at least get the helm to turn around. Ken watched as slowly the boat made a wide turn, then came back onto the reverse of track that they had previously been on. The sun wasn't reflecting off the sea and everything looked like a dull grey.

'What was the colour? What was the colour of who went in?' asked the second officer, having returned.

'White and black. It was like a white and black flash,' said Ken.

'The master's launching the rescue boats, won't be long.'

Ken tried to keep his eyes on where he had seen the figure in the water, but it was getting harder. The second officer took some details off him, and was working out timings and positions. Ken could see that the rescue boats were about to be dispatched.

'Where the hell's Jenny?' asked one of his crewmates, looking to deploy one of the boats.

'The call's gone out, she should be here. There's a bloody rescue; where is she?'

'She'd just come up to the deck, I just saw her. She was coming off shift, then going up on deck.'

The second officer turned to a crew member, despatching them for Jenny. Ken watched the water but the figure he'd seen before was now out of sight. When the despatch runner had returned, the second officer stiffened up slightly and then turned to address the crew around him.

'We're looking for Jenny Trimble. Jenny Trimble is missing.'

Ken felt the sickness in his stomach. No, this couldn't be right. This couldn't happen. His eyes scoured the water, gazing here, there, and everywhere, but it all looked the same. There wasn't anyone there. Ken continued to watch.

At first, the helicopter arrived, then other vessels and a lifeboat. The things he had seen, the time he'd seen them at were reconfirmed by the first officer but after that, Ken was left gripping his hands on the balcony rail and looking down into the sea, hoping to find Jenny. But in truth, there was little chance.

Chapter 13

Macleod had to pick up a flight from Stornoway to Glasgow as Minchlines ferries had begun to get calls from the press asking if there was a murderer on board. Macleod had instantly gone to Jona to ask which of her staff knew about the needle in the body of Daphne Walsh, but Jona defended her people fiercely, saying that nothing had leaked out.

Macleod knew Jona Nakamura; he knew she wouldn't have leaked anything. He was also aware that she'd come down hard on anyone who had even thought about it. Although the obvious place to start, Macleod also thought of those working with him. He had kept the idea of murder amongst his top team, and certainly, none of them would have given any offhand remark to involve the press. He decided he would go to the press conference to find out what the lay of the land was and to back up the ferry company who'd been particularly helpful.

On arrival in Glasgow, Macleod had been picked up by a local constable and taken directly to a small hotel. In one of the rooms, a small stage was set up with a number of chairs in front of it for the press. Macleod was taken through to another room at the rear where he shook hands with the chairman of

Minchlines ferries.

'I can't believe we're getting all this heat,' the man said. 'All tales of murderers on the ferries. Can you imagine what that's going to do for our business? I hope you'll be able to issue a full and frank rebuttal of that idea,' the man said.

'I'd like to be able to,' said Macleod. 'Truly, I would, but that's not going to happen.'

'What? Why not? You're investigating these things. We brought you in to investigate, to point out there wasn't anything wrong.'

'With all due respect, I was brought in to find out if there was anything wrong and I'm afraid there is. We've kept it close to ourselves.'

'Not close enough,' said the man, 'clearly. Why wasn't I informed?'

'Because of this. You would be panicked. A panic from you could spread to everyone else. At the moment, we believe one of the people who died in the overboard situations was actually murdered. The others are much more difficult to prove seeing as some of the bodies are still in the sea. It's a terrible situation.'

'Terrible it is. One of our own this time. Jenny Trimble.'

'Did you know her?' asked Macleod.

'Only met her once,' said the man in the seat opposite. 'Once was enough. Striking woman. Very striking.'

Macleod didn't quite know how to take that comment but instead looked to see the doors of the room beginning to open.

'If there's a murderer onboard, Macleod, should we stop running?'

'No,' said Macleod. 'Why? Why would you stop running?'

'To prevent more deaths.'

'If we had a murderer here in the city, what? We just close

everywhere down? We just don't do anything? No, you need to keep running. You've got lifeline services.'

'But if this publicity continues,' said the CEO. 'It's not going to be good for us, is it? It's not going to be good for the business.'

'We are working on it and we're getting there.'

'What am I meant to say when we walk out here?'

'You refer the questions to me,' said Macleod. 'I'll take care of them.'

A woman walked up to the CEO and announced that they were ready for them next door. Macleod followed the man through the doors onto the platform with a large number of camera flashes around him. He was well used to it. Macleod sat down behind a line of tables awaiting the CEO to take charge of the proceedings. The man took a moment to stand and drink some water before announcing that the press conference was open. Almost immediately, the first question came in.

'With the number of deaths on the ferry and the recent disappearance of one of your own colleagues, is it true that the ferries have got a murderer on board?'

'Now, let's not get ahead of ourselves,' said the CEO. 'There's no evidence that there is any murderer on board. There's no . . .'

Macleod put his hand across in front of the CEO. 'Excuse me. I'll advise if there's a murderer onboard or not. Please, I'll take this question.'

Macleod rose to his feet, staring down the press contingent. If there was one thing he hated, it was these vultures. Sure, they sometimes could be helpful if you were looking for a missing person, but so many of them were melodramatic with it that the actual information seemed to get lost to the general public.

'If I can just set the record straight,' said Macleod. 'First off, there have been a number of deaths on various ferries belonging to the Minchlines company. We are investigating those at this time ascertaining whether they were suicide or if some other party was at work. Currently, we cannot confirm a third party being involved.'

Macleod knew that wasn't strictly true. There was convincing evidence that a third party was involved if not confirmed but the wording made it sound a lot more vague and that the police were still investigating. The last thing Macleod wanted any potential murderer to know was that he was on to them.

'Does this mean that the ferries will be shutting down? If you have a murderer running amok, Inspector?'

'Just a moment,' said Macleod. 'That comment is loose and wild and will only lead to the general public being scared.'

'Are they safe then? Are the ferries safe?'

'At this moment in time,' said Macleod, 'we're investigating, ascertaining what has happened in these circumstances.'

'So what? In the meantime, we all have to risk being on board with a potential murderer.'

'I reiterate to you that we are investigating. At this time, I believe the ferries will continue to run. Is that correct?' Macleod turned to the CEO beside him. He simply nodded. 'I think we need a bit of calm.'

'Can you give us the odds of there being a murderer on board?' said a male journalist. 'Is it more there is, or more that there isn't?'

'I'm not at liberty to say that,' said Macleod.

'Well, we're here to try and find out for our readers whether it's safe to be on a ferry. Can you say it's safe to be on a ferry?'

'That would be a crazy comment,' said Macleod. 'Is it safe to be on a road? Is it safe to be up in a plane? What do you mean by safe?'

'It means, are we all going to get murdered.'

Macleod could feel all the hairs in his neck rising and anger seething through him. He'd given a sensible statement. All they had to do was just leave it there. *Why did the press always have to come on and go for the jugular?* Macleod was sweating but tried not to show it. *If only Hope was here. She was better at the press. Either Hope or Clarissa. Clarissa would chew them up and spit them out. Although she'd probably cause a serious incident at the same time.*

'I reiterate again the investigations are continuing.'

'Are the ferries safe, Inspector?'

'I told you, I can't answer that. It's not a question that has any level of appreciation of the situation.'

'Would you suggest that people don't go up on deck on their own?'

Of course, they'd interviewed all these passengers. Some of the questions were bound to come back. Did you see someone alone? Did you see them up there? Was anyone else about? The press would soon find out from the interviewees.

'Once again, Inspector, is it safe to be on the ferries?'

Macleod bit his lip. He wanted to say, 'Come over here and I'll give you a good clip around the ear for being such a clown and stirring up the public.' On the other hand, they were right. There was a murderer on the ferries.

'Various coincidences are being investigated thoroughly by my officers. As soon as we have something, we will brief you.'

'At some appropriate junction,' Macleod said in his head, because without it, the statement would probably be a lie. The press were the last people he briefed.

'That's a no then. We're not safe in the ferries. They've got a murderer.' The room began to break into an uproar. Macleod sat down. He hated the press. He really did.

* * *

Laura had only been on the lifeboat crew less than a month. That was when she got her qualification and was able to be part of the search crew. She stood up on the deck of the lifeboat, looking out across the water. The waves kept going up and down, making it hard to see each part of the sea as the helicopter passed over ahead. Other vessels were making way here and there, nobody seeing anything except for the blue.

In truth, they were probably looking for a body, especially in this cold water. The victim had been in for too long, although there had been cases of people surviving longer. The casualty had entered the water in what seemed like an uncontrolled fashion. They'd also had no life jacket and who knew how well they could swim.

The coxswain turned the lifeboat back as it began another straight-line search through the water, Laura and her colleagues looking out, trying to spot anything that was untoward. The vessel, now routing the other direction, became bumpier as it chopped through the water. Laura hung on with one hand when she tried to look through binoculars with the other. She'd bring them up every now and again, but most of the searching was done with the bare eye.

Laura thought she saw something in the water, something that moved. She pointed with her finger. 'There,' she cried. 'Something over there.'

'Whereabouts?'

'Turn about one hundred and thirty-five degrees.'

'Have you got eyes on?'

Laura watched the waves go up and down. She did have eyes on. Then she didn't and then she did. The lifeboat turned quickly and started to make towards where Laura pointed. As they got closer, they could see a figure in the water. The coxswain called to the crew to prepare to bring the casualty onboard, and they reached out with long poles, dragging the floating victim towards them. As they pulled her onboard, they could see it was a woman dressed in a ferry uniform.

Laura could hear the cox calling for the helicopter to drop down their paramedic while two of the team began to work on Jenny Trimble's body. However, there seemed little hope. She wasn't breathing when they brought her on and she still wasn't breathing several minutes later while the winchman above was descending. It only took the winchman paramedic less than a minute to confirm that Jenny Trimble was deceased. Within another five minutes, he was back up in the helicopter, which was now routing for its base. The lifeboat turned back towards shore and Jenny Trimble's body, placed inside a black bag, was carried down below. They would rendezvous on the shore where a coroner would pick up the body.

* * *

Macleod was back in the room behind the press stage and fending off some difficult questions from the CEO of Minchlines. His phone began to ring and he gave a silent prayer of thanks as he excused himself from the man and strode over to the far corner of the room.

'Sir, it's Ross. I think we need to get Jona on down to Oban.'

'Why?' asked Macleod. 'Something come up?'

'Jenny Trimble's come up. We just heard that they've found her. I've asked the undertaker to keep the body to one side and not to touch it.'

'Good work, Ross. Get yourself down there as well and join Jona. Quick as you can. Take some statements, find out what happened. I'm going to head back up to Inverness. Once I find out how Hope and Clarissa have gone on, we'll start to work out where to go with this investigation. In the meantime, I want all details about what happened on that Islay ferry.'

'Of course,' said Ross. 'I'll try and speak to you tonight.'

Macleod closed the call, hung his head low for a moment, and then walked over to the CEO of Minchlines. The man began to hassle the Inspector.

'Macleod, explain how this business is meant to work. What have you done by not confirming there was no murderer onboard?'

Macleod put his hand up in front of the man, stopping him in his tracks. 'Look, I've got some bad news for you. They've just found Jenny Trimble's body. The good news from our point of view is because we found it, we can find out if she was murdered.'

'Dear God,' said the CEO. 'Can you believe this? Can you believe this?'

In all his years as a policeman, Macleod knew the extent to which people would go to kill. He could believe it very, very easily. Rather than lie to the man, he simply replied, 'It can be hard to believe. That's true.'

Chapter 14

H ope gratefully stepped out of the little green sports car onto a Glasgow side street. Looking up at the tall building in front of her, she stretched. At six feet tall, she towered over Clarissa and was not designed for the passenger seat of a small sports car. The drive up from the south felt like a long one and Hope had tried to think through what had happened so far on the case. Were these doctors the answer? She wasn't sure, but hopefully, she'd find out.

As Clarissa fed some money into a parking metre, Hope walked over to the front door of the building before her and saw the sign for Dr Stevens's marital counselling. She pressed the intercom, and advised who she was, before the door buzzed open. Slowly, she climbed two flights of stairs, Clarissa behind her, huffing and puffing, and complaining about the lack of a lift, but for Hope, there were no such worries. Finally getting to stretch out her legs was a blessing, not a curse.

The door that presented itself to them on the second floor was simple enough, a brown affair with a dour plaque on it, simply spelling out, once again, Dr Stevens Marital Counselling. Hope knocked on the door and heard a, 'Come in.' Inside, a secretary offered Hope a seat saying that the doctor would be with her very shortly and asking whether they would like a cup of tea or coffee. Hope passed, but Clarissa eagerly grabbed a coffee, reminding Hope of Macleod, that the older detectives seemed to live off the stuff.

It took another two minutes before they were shown into an office with a desk on one side and a small set of sofas in the other corner. Dr Stevens was almost as tall as Hope but was of a skinnier configuration. She looked tall and elegant with brown hair that had some white streaks running through it. She wore a black jacket with a long pencil skirt and a white blouse. Hope noted the heart locket hanging from around her neck.

'Thank you for seeing us, doctor. I'm Detective Sergeant Hope McGrath. This is Detective Sergeant Clarissa Urquhart. I hope we aren't disturbing you, but we need some information about some of your clients.'

'Well, I hope I can give it to you,' said Dr Stevens. 'There is client confidentiality.'

'Said client is dead, so I'm hoping that won't be a problem.'

'Is their partner or spouse still alive?'

'Yes, they are, but we're actually running a murder investigation, so anything you can tell us would be gratefully received.'

'That's understood, but my first duty is to my clients,' said Dr Stevens.

'Andrew Culshaw,' said Clarissa, 'he was a client of yours, wasn't he?'

'The Culshaws? Yes, terrible tragedy falling off the ferry.'

'You said, "falling off,"' said Hope. 'You don't believe he committed suicide then?'

'Well, I'm just saying what I know. He fell off the ferry. Did he jump? I don't know. Was he pushed? I'm beginning to wonder because you're here.'

Hope thought the woman was fairly smart, not giving away anything, choosing her words wisely. 'What can you tell us about the Culshaws?'

'Well, Andrew Culshaw was a highly volatile figure. He believed he had a right to everything, including his wife and the way she behaved. He would constantly get into trouble because people would deny him that he felt entitled to. He would simply demand things. In some ways, he was mentally unstable.'

'You said he felt he had a right to everything; where did that come from?' asked Clarissa.

'I think he thought it was God-given and I mean that in the genuine sense. He felt that he was owed it. God had put him here. He certainly was like that with his wife, seemed to think she was property. I tried to dissuade him of that, tried to let her show what she thought, but he was a very difficult case.'

'How do you show him that side?' asked Hope. 'Forgive me, I'm not very experienced. I've had a couple of partners, not been in a marriage, and I'm quite intrigued to know.'

'Well, I knew only too well,' said Dr Stevens. 'I'm divorced at fifty-five now as well. I learnt the hard way. If someone wants to take everything in the marriage, it doesn't work. That's what I tried to show him, show him the effect he was having on his wife. It took time. It took a lot of patience from her.'

'Is she a patient person?' asked Clarissa.

'In my opinion, she is. The woman is probably free of a lot now. Though I don't know . . . She stayed with him because she really did want him. That was the sad thing, he didn't need to have ownership of her. She was there with him, but the way he went about it made her life hell, and that's why they ended up with me. Although it took a long time for her to get him to come. She came alone for the first four or five sessions.'

'You say he wrecked the marriage? It very much was all him, was it?'

'Completely, she's a decent soul.'

'Yet, he came off the ferry,' said Clarissa. 'They were both on the ferry at the time. Is there any chance that Mrs Culshaw would have done it?'

'Mrs Culshaw? Mrs Culshaw couldn't lift me out of this room. Could she throw someone off a ferry the size of her husband, I doubt it. I really do. I don't think she'd have the inclination either. She cared for him. She worshipped him. She just wanted him to change. I don't think it's really a sensible option.'

'She couldn't have snapped or anything, do you think?'

'No, she wasn't near to that point, very rational woman.'

'Apparently, they were arguing just before it all happened. I'm just wondering if she could have lost it with him,' offered Hope.

'No. No way. They argued a lot all the time. Andrew was unbelievable. If she did something, she did it wrong. It didn't matter what it was. He wouldn't have done it that way, and often, even if she managed to do it his way, he was complaining because he had never asked her to do it in the first place. It could be as little as how she set her hair. There was definitely a mental issue within the man. Definitely.

'However, it was very hard to get at because he wouldn't spend time with me. In a lot of ways, he ruined her life. She should have walked from him ages ago, but she wouldn't; she couldn't. I guess I know a bit about that, but that was some time ago.

'Look I don't want to rush you either,' said Dr Stevens, 'but I've got dinner arrangements and so I'm going to have to depart sometime soon. So, if you just keep your questions coming, I'll do my best. Anything I can't answer here and now, obviously, I'll get back to you.'

'She had said they were on a trip away on the ferry,' said Hope. 'Was that normal for him to take her away or for her to go with him?'

'Absolutely. For all that they argued and bickered, they were never apart. As I said, she did worship him in a lot of ways even though he made her life a misery.'

'Why on earth do people do that?' said Clarissa. 'I don't understand that.'

'I'm sure you don't,' said Dr Stevens. 'You seem like quite a formidable woman.'

Hope rolled her eyes. It was only too true. Clarissa, for all that she was, a tour de force, Macleod's rottweiler didn't have a lot of sympathy for people who didn't cope.

'We'll try and be snappy as we can,' said Hope. 'We're off to see a Dr Jacobs who's in a similar line of work as you, do you know him?'

'Yes, I do. We met at a conference but that's as far as I know him.'

'Very good,' said Hope. 'Would you know of any reason why Andrew Culshaw was being targeted by anyone?'

'What do you mean?' asked the woman.

'Targeted enough to be killed. It would be someone who had planned it.'

'Do you think he was killed?' asked Dr Stevens.

'We do think it, but we can't prove it. Unfortunately, Andrew's body's never come back to us; otherwise, we might be able to. They may have used Ketamine, large dose.'

'Well, it's definitely not Marie Culshaw then. She can't stand needles; she can't use them. She'd been a mess trying to do that. Definitely not her. And with his nature, who knows who Andrew may have annoyed?'

'How did you feel about your clients?' asked Clarissa.

'How do you mean?' asked Dr Stevens.

'Well, you see these poor wretches come in, people like Marie; do you feel sorry for them?'

'I'm sure I do in the same way that you feel sorry for people who are victims, but you also have a professional duty to do the best for everyone. I was trying to help Andrew as much as Marie. I mean, you get that, don't you? If somebody pulls a gun, you try and disarm them, you don't just obliterate them to save the innocent party standing beside them.'

'Indeed,' said Clarissa, 'but sometimes push comes to shove, doesn't it?'

'I don't know what you mean by that,' said Dr Stevens.

'I just wonder how you feel seeing all these things. Is this merely mind games to you, as something to be successfully mastered, or do you actually feel for these people?'

'I am human,' said Stevens, 'but in here I maintain a professional detachment. Now, if you'll excuse me, I really do have to get on for dinner. Is there anything else?'

'Can you let us have access to some of the notes, the times of the visits, et cetera?'

'Of course, but the actual meeting notes, I want to be here to discuss with you if you need them.'

'I'm not sure we will do that at the moment but we're just looking for possible outside connections to Andrew. Anybody else that might have had a grievance against Andrew Culshaw.'

'Of course, you just talk to my secretary; that won't be a problem. I'm sorry I have to rush you, but I really do need to be going.'

Hope stood up with Clarissa, and Dr Stevens showed them out to her secretary outside. While the pair of them stood with the secretary making notes about who had appointments around the same time as the Culshaws, Hope noticed Dr Stevens depart the building. She had a scarf around her neck and had changed her skirt and jacket into something that looked even smarter. She gave the pair a quick wave as she left the office. Five minutes later, Hope and Clarissa were downstairs about to get into Clarissa's car.

'I'm not sure what we learnt from that,' said Hope, but Clarissa tapped her on the shoulder. 'Walk with me now.' Hope followed Clarissa down a small side alley where Clarissa stopped and turned around, peering around the corner. 'For someone being off to dinner, she's coming back.'

'Are you sure? She went down the street. Is it definitely her?' asked Hope.

'Trust me, she doesn't look like she's got a happy face. Let's bump into her.' Clarissa marched back out of the alley and met Dr Stevens as she arrived at the front door to her office.

'I thought you were off to dinner,' said Clarissa.

'It has just been cancelled, unfortunately, so I thought I'd come back and do a little bit more work. Was my secretary able to get you everything you needed?'

'Yes, she did. Not a problem,' said Hope. 'I think we've got everything. I'm not sure we need to disturb you again. As I said, we've got to meet at Dr Jacobs.'

'He works out of Aberdeen; how are you meeting here?' asked Dr Stevens.

'He's stopping down in a hotel. Apparently, he's got some meetings, but has agreed to say "hello" to us.'

'Very good. Don't let me detain you,' said Dr Stevens. 'Like I say, if you need anything else, please reach out to me.'

'Will do,' said Hope and watched as the woman made her way to the front door of the office. Her feet seemed leaden; her shoulders slumped.

'She's pretty disappointed, isn't she?' said Clarissa. 'Anyway, onwards. If we're going to meet Dr Jacobs, we're going to need to get a move on.'

'That's all right,' said Hope. 'Remember, this is Glasgow; you can't drive like a maniac around here.'

'Who was driving like a maniac?'

'On the way up here put me in mind of making sure I get with Ross next time.'

'That would leave Seoras with me; that's not going to work, is it? He's petrified of me.'

'He's petrified of you in a car, and I don't blame him.'

'Enough,' said Clarissa. 'Get in. You're only complaining because of those long legs of yours. I can't believe you complain about them either. If I had legs like that, I'd happily display them.'

'You're not really women's lib, are you?'

Clarissa laughed. 'I don't need to be freed,' said Clarissa. 'I've been dominating men most of my life.'

She laughed loudly as she rounded the car and got in at the driver's side. Hope carefully stepped into the car, pulling her legs up tight, wishing she'd more room to stretch them out. It was dawning on Hope that she hadn't really worked with Clarissa much. Usually, Macleod was with her, or else, she was off with Ross. Hope was beginning to understand why

Macleod liked her. He seemed to like women who had a bit of fire in them. Jane was like that as well.

He seems to view me slightly differently, thought Hope. *Maybe that's a good thing.* Hope reached around the back of her head making sure that her ponytail was secure with a borrowed hair tie, and then quickly put her belt on as Clarissa pulled out into the Glasgow traffic. Hope nearly swore as a number of car horns were sounded, all aimed at the little green machine that was now racing across Glasgow to their next meeting.

Chapter 15

Alan Ross stared around the room where the ferry crew had gathered. They had brought in the reserve crew who should've started next week, and they were preparing the ship to depart but Ross had noticed even with them, there was a large degree of unease. The oncoming master had said there were a number of sicknesses that had come on suddenly, and Ross had the general feeling that the situation was beginning to get out of control.

Jenny Trimble's body, having been recovered, was now at the local morgue, with Jona Nakamura in attendance. She would come back with her findings soon enough, but in the meantime, Ross had taken charge of a small detachment of constables from the local area to interview the crew. Initially, they'd started with the passengers, but there was little to be found from them. They didn't know Jenny Trimble. Sure, they'd seen her working in the shop, but that was it. Nobody had been up on deck to see her, and so from the time of her going up on deck until she hit the water was still a complete mystery. Ross understood one thing, that while finding out what happened in that time may provide some sort of explanation, what was going to stop these crimes was finding out the link between all the victims, how they were being selected.

Jenny Trimble had worked the ferry for a number of years. Ross had found that out from her records, but he wanted to know what sort of person she was. A constable had been dispatched to her husband to advise him of her demise and also to see if he could find any details. She wasn't an old woman by any stretch of the imagination, just arriving to her thirties, and Ross thought her slightly different to some of the others. But then, they were all different, weren't they? There were heterosexual couples, homosexual couples, but they're always couples, he thought, and couples with problems.

Ross watched the constables begin to work their way round the room, taking aside a crew member at a time and asking questions. Ross would soon pore over the statements and verify what was being said, but he watched one woman being particularly talkative. She was diminutive in figure, but she seemed to have a mouth that made up for it and he wondered if it ever could fall silent. The rest of the crew seemed to be in shock that made them withdraw but this woman seemed to erupt because of the fright she'd had.

Ross wandered over and listened to the woman for a few moments before tapping the constable on the shoulder. 'I'll take this lady through to a different room. I want to take a full statement from her.'

The constable nodded and spoke to the woman, advising her to follow Ross into the next room.

Inside there was a bare table and Ross turned to find the coffee machine and fetch what he thought was the weakest-looking coffee he'd ever seen in his life. *It shouldn't be that colour*, he thought. But he placed a plastic cup in front of the woman who was now sitting down on a chair but still talking.

'Woah. Hold on,' said Ross. 'Let's just start over again. I'm Detective Constable Alan Ross, and I'll be taking a statement. Your name is?'

'Anna Chain. Yes, as in like what you do with a bike. You chain it up to something. Don't ask me how I married a Mr Chain.'

'And you knew Jenny Trimble quite well?'

'We've been working this ferry for three years together. We knew each other. She would come and chat to me. Pop into my quarters if she was bored.'

'What was Jenny like?' asked Ross.

'What was Jenny like?' said the woman back to him. 'You can ask anyone here, Jenny liked to put it about. Jenny liked to flirt and be adored and have a good time. That was Jenny. Don't get me wrong, she was fun to be about. Quick tongue and a funny one with it, but not a stable sort of person.'

'Did she know you thought that of her?'

'Well, I told her often enough. Probably just needs to settle down but she never did. I think Jenny regretted being married.'

'What's the name of her husband? Did you ever meet him?'

'No, but she told me a lot about him, Robbie. Very staid guy, she said. Very traditional. Liked a woman who was demure. Not in her place, don't get me wrong; the guy wasn't an ogre or anything—he was just a lot calmer than Jenny. Well, at least that's how she put it. Apparently, she found him at a wedding, and he fell for her and they got married quickly, within six weeks. After a year, she was bored of him, and she was off finding other people.'

'So, you said she slept around?'

'Yes, that's right,' said Anna.

'Okay, did she sleep around on the vessel?'

124

'I shouldn't really say this, but yes. I mean, I'd never admit it to the bosses.'

'That's fine,' said Ross. 'You just need to admit it to me. Who did she sleep with?'

'Well, there was George, but he's not on this cycle. She jumped into bed with him a few times. Then there was Sally.'

'So, she didn't really have a preference?'

'She was mainly men, but yes. I think she just liked to experiment; that was her words. Well, that's what she told me. I didn't ask too much if you understand.'

'Oh, of course,' said Ross. 'If she felt this bad though, why didn't she just leave her husband?'

'Oh, she said to me that she'd asked him several times for a divorce, but he wouldn't have it. He was afraid of the shame of it. He was almost happier to let her run around making a fool of him in some ways.'

'And Sally? Is she on at the moment?'

'No, she got off just before this run. That's the thing, if you're looking for people that she actually had been with, they're not on the boat at the moment. The other person she liked was Ken.'

'Ken who?'

'Ken MacNeil. He's got a big family, loads of kids. Lovely guy, Ken. You can't help but like Ken. I think Jenny liked him in a lot of respects. He is a funny guy; he can make good jokes, but she obviously saw the fact he had a lot of children too. I think she liked that about him. Thought that must mean something, whatever that means,' said Anna, looking away. 'She was a bit of a nutjob. I know it's probably wrong to say that of the dead, but she was a nutter, an attractive nutter. She knew how to entice; I'll give her that.'

'It's funny how you talk about her because you said you were friends.'

'Boat friends. I wouldn't be doing anything with her off this boat,' said Anna. 'There's no way. But here, what can we do? You sit and you natter. She wasn't interested in me physically, which is fine so, therefore, her tales and stories, they were quite fun to listen to. It does get a bit monotonous on this boat. Back and forward seeing the customers, not happy with this bit of food or delighted with this. 'Oh look, it's choppy today.' You know, you get all the normal tales and then you got what Jenny told you. She'd tell me about all her sexual exploits from the previous weeks when she was off the ship. It was fun; I was bored. I'll miss her from that point of view. Certainly, wouldn't have wanted to see her go like this.'

'Can I ask? Do you know if Jenny and her husband saw any professional help?'

'Professional help? I think they did. Jenny occasionally would be off the boat for twenty-four hours. You might have to ask the master about that. She said it was because she had to go somewhere with her husband. She never told me what it was. In honesty, she seemed nearly a little bit embarrassed by it.'

Ross nodded and began to think.

'Where were you when Jenny disappeared?'

'I was up in the canteen. It's where I work, preparing. You can ask anyone. The chef, everybody there. I was in there the whole time.'

'Okay, Anna. Would anybody on this vessel want to harm Jenny?'

'I don't think so. She got on well with everyone. I mean, obviously, there's the two she got intimate with, but outside of that everybody liked Jenny. I mean, she was nice-looking, she was a lot of fun, and like I say, you didn't actually have to go anywhere with her. We're just work colleagues here, so that was okay. I mean, to be out with her in public, I mean on a night out or whatever, I can imagine she'd be quite shocking. I'm not sure everybody here would take that. You know what though?' said Anna. 'It's really sad. She had everything, in a lot of ways. She could have any man she wanted if she toned herself down a bit or just been a bit faithful. She could've, but she just couldn't handle herself. It's a real shame. Genuine, lovely person. She actually cared at times too, but she couldn't keep her libido in check, always wanted a bit more. Maybe it was her husband. Maybe he couldn't, well, you know. It's weird talking about people like this, isn't it? I guess that's at the core of some people's lives.'

Ross took down the woman's address and thanked her for her candour before letting her depart. When he stepped back out into the main room, the constables were over halfway through the crew but Ross called the master aside, taking him into the room previously occupied by himself and Anna.

The man was in his fifties and looked somewhat ashamed.

'I know why you've brought me through,' he said, 'but it was once and once only.'

Ross sat down, his coffee still untouched to his left-hand side. 'I haven't brought you through for anything except to ask some questions,' said Ross. 'What are you talking about?'

'Well, Jenny, you know how she was. I'm sure they've told you. Well, me and Jenny at one point.'

'You had sexual relations with a member of the crew?'

'I know it sounds bad when you put it like that. Certainly don't want my bosses to find out, but it was once and once

127

only. It wasn't really me she was after; she just liked the idea of doing it on the bridge. It was when we were weather-bound for a day.'

'Does anybody else know about this?'

'Well, she'd have told somebody, but the crew wouldn't let on. Most of them probably think it's a rumour or something that Jenny just made up. She was lively and vivacious, I was having a hard time and well, she offered. Not proud of it. I'm really not proud of it, but also know I was up on the bridge. I was in sight of everyone when she went into the water.'

'Okay. What I really wanted to ask you was, Jenny took time off according to one of your colleagues, twenty-four hours at a time on occasions. What was that for?'

'Medical appointment,' said the man. 'It's a medical appointment, except she told me it was to do with counselling. Her and her husband. She had brought me a form in for the appointment just to try and prove it, which I didn't ask for. I think she was indignant about it, that's why she was giving me the form. Wanted me to tell her that she didn't need counselling.'

'Did she require counselling?'

'She required a lobotomy. She was so full-on. Jenny was nuts. Really likable girl, but my goodness, she was crackers, but good at pulling you into her way of thinking. Very full-on. Could turn a man's head as I've said.'

'Do you know which medical professional they were seeing?'

'Dr Jacobs. I remember that because I always associated it with crackers, the ones you eat, and she was crackers. I know it's daft, but it's funny how the brain sticks things in your head, isn't it?'

'So, Dr Jacobs. That's useful. Thank you.'

'Do we know who did this?' asked the master.

'Not yet. It doesn't look like it was any of the crew.'

'There's been a number of these deaths now. Our crew are worried, I'm worried. I mean, you don't expect to work a ferry and start losing members of crew or passengers. Happens once. Well, you know, people do things. They jump off ferries, there's accidents, arguments. There's too many now. This is going to scare people. Not just my crew—it's going to scare passengers.'

'I'm well aware of that, sir. We're going to try and get to the bottom this quickly.'

'It's all different ferries. That's crazy, isn't it? All these different ferries. Are they just grabbing people and throwing them over?'

Ross wanted to tell him no, Ross wanted to tell him that actually, it looked like it was couples. As long as you weren't having any problems and seeing doctors, you were probably all right, but he didn't. He simply stood up, shook his head, and advised the man that inquiries were still proceeding.

Chapter 16

Macleod stepped out of the Detective Chief Inspector's office and could feel the sweat on his head. That had been a lot of questioning, even for an experienced hand like himself, and having been involved in the conference call with the ferry company and members of the Scottish Parliament, he felt he needed to sit down for a couple of minutes. His team were deployed here, there, and everywhere for such was the nature of the crime. He didn't even have the smiling face of Ross there, building him back up, ever a protector of his boss, and one thoroughly efficient man.

Macleod made his way back to the main office where a couple of constables were working their way through some data for him but otherwise, the office was empty. None of his three colleagues were there, and when he went over to the coffee machine, he found it wasn't even on. *Some things just won't do*, he thought.

He wanted to be back out on the road with the team, but he had got pulled into talking to higher-up authorities and Macleod hated it. He liked being in charge, liked being the main dog in the office, able to send people here, there, and wherever. What he didn't like was being on the end of a leash, brought in by the DCI to answer the questions that, really, he felt his boss should be dealing with.

His boss had only entered the role, replacing a woman Macleod had seen as a competent person, but now he had no rapport with the man who was currently in that position. He was younger than Macleod and Macleod wondered just how much detecting he'd done, for he seemed to be a lot more about image and how things would play out amongst the public. Macleod had always thought murder was about finding who was responsible.

He cleaned out the coffee machine, put some freshly ground coffee into it, filled it with water, and stayed beside it as it dripped through. He listened to it gurgle, sniffing in the aroma as the water passed through the coffee, urging it on so he could pour out a cup of the liquid below.

Ross would be getting on with it. He thought of his junior colleague and realised this was the first time he'd let Ross loose since that time on the Monach Isles. The poor guy had almost ended up dead, but he'd done well uncovering a major drug operation in the most extreme of circumstances. *It was about time that Ross made sergeant,* thought Macleod. *It was about time that he stepped up. The man needed to think about his career.*

Ross was that efficient person, the person that was keeping Macleod afloat in some ways, covering all the bases underneath, the little details that Macleod would never get round to. *The trouble with people like that,* thought Macleod, *is they're too useful. They get kept there. They are never allowed to show their real potential.*

Kirsten had been very similar in the sense that she could handle all the details, but she'd gone on and ended up working

131

for the Special Services. In some ways, Macleod thought it a success, certainly in career terms, even if he wasn't overly keen about Kirsten actually working for such a dark organisation. The woman had a good heart and a lot of integrity, and Macleod sometimes wondered just how that fitted in.

Ross was the same and Macleod really should be starting to check up on him, make sure the guy didn't need any more help. He walked into his office once the coffee had been poured, sat down behind his desk, and opened up his laptop. Now, Ross had said to click this icon over here, then to make sure that these other boxes were checked. Macleod did so, then found that nothing was opening up properly. He reached inside his jacket pocket, took out his phone, and dialled Ross's number.

'Sir,' said Ross, 'can I help you?'

'How are you getting on down there? Everything okay?'

'We've been going through all the passengers, and we've just finished the crew. It appears our Jenny Trimble was a flirt. Had issues with her husband, very similar to some of our other victims.'

'Tell me more,' said Macleod.

'Well, I've just had a constable come back from talking to her husband. He said Jenny was unfaithful to him and they were getting help. I know it's from a Dr Jacobs. That's the same person the Walshes were seeing. Jenny Trimble was sexually active with a number of people after becoming bored with her husband, but her husband wouldn't give up on her, said she needed treatment, needed to deal with what he saw as an addiction.

'She was seeing two other people on the vessel, but they weren't on board at the time the incident happened. It's looking very similar to what happened before. I'm expecting

Jona to call in a minute. Do you want to come off the phone, sir, and we'll go into the video chat and the three of us can talk together?'

'Good idea,' said Macleod. 'I was going to video chat to you anyway, but it won't open again.'

'Did you tick the second box down?' asked Ross.

'Second? Thought it was the third.'

'No, we talked about this. That's not the one, it's the second one.'

'You should write this down for me,' said Macleod, and then he saw Ross's eyes narrow. Yes, Ross was right. Macleod should write it down every time, but he felt that with regard to the computers, he'd have a book of written notes that would accompany him everywhere. He grew up in a time of typewriters for goodness sake.

Macleod put down the call and made the adjustments to the screen and was speaking to Ross again within two minutes.

'You can see me now, sir. Is that correct?'

'Yes, I can. When's Jona joining us?'

'Any minute now.' Macleod sat patiently sipping some of his coffee.

'Do you know, Ross, that I came back today out of a meeting with the DCI and there was no coffee on the go?'

'Well, no, sir, there won't be. I tend to put the coffee on. Failing that, Clarissa does it. If we weren't there, Hope would do it.'

'But I've got two constables here helping out on the case, working from the office; they didn't put it on either.'

'Well no, they won't,' said Ross.

'Why?' asked Macleod.

'It's your coffee. They know you; they don't touch your

coffee.'

'What do you mean they don't touch my coffee? They can make the coffee.'

'No, they can't,' said Ross. 'You're very particular about your coffee and to be quite honest, I think they're scared they'll get it wrong.'

'Scared they'll get it wrong? I'll give them scared to get it wrong, lazy good-for-nothings. They can make the coffee.'

'When was the last time you made the coffee, sir?' asked Ross.

'Just now.'

'But before that?'

Macleod thought back; he was struggling, really struggling.

'You don't make the coffee,' said Ross; 'we make the coffee. We know how to make the coffee for you. You would complain about the coffee if it was made by other people.'

Macleod sat back and simply nodded. More and more, he seemed to be under attack by the team over the small things. They never questioned the way he led an investigation or what he was doing, but things on the periphery: how to drive, how to make coffee, and he wasn't sure if this was them being on a different level of comfort with him, or whether he was losing his authority. The appearance of Jona Nakamura on the screen broke his train of thought.

'Good, Jona, how's Jenny Trimble?'

'Well, she's dead,' said Jona.

There we go again, he thought. 'You know what I mean, Jona.'

'Sorry, Seoras, she's very similar to our other victim, she's been dosed up with a large amount of ketamine, the date rape drug. Once again, it looks like it's a massive dose, would have caused paralysis, she'd not be able to move, but she would have been awake hitting the water. There's no physical damage to her, she simply drowned. It's quite scary, you could tip her up and over, leave her hanging off the edge of the ferry, although I doubt they did that.'

'No,' said Macleod, 'they'd want to do it quick. If you're on your own up there, you would do it quick. Would she respond?'

'Respond?' queried Jona. 'What do you mean exactly?'

'You say it puts them in a state of paralysis. Would they give a facial reaction or anything if they were hung over the edge? Would the killer be able to look at them and think, 'Oh yes, they're panicking; they're scared?''

'No,' said Jona, 'but they'd know they were awake. They could also tell them exactly why they were being killed.'

'Why don't we start looking at the ketamine side of it? We know two of them have been paralysed this way so, therefore, maybe that could be a lead,' said Ross.

'It's not that difficult to get hold of, Ross, though,' said Macleod, 'but if you think there's a chance to trace it.'

'Well, if Jona can get samples out of the body, I'll see what I can do. It's a long shot but sometimes these things are worth pursuing.'

'Indeed. How long are you going to be down there?' Macleod asked.

'We still need to wrap up, I'm not sure how long Jona is going to be here either.'

'We've been over the ferry, forensic-wise, can't find anything, I'm just about done with the body; we'll start moving back up to Inverness shortly.'

'I'll try and come up tomorrow, sir,' said Ross.

'And I'll try and have the coffee on,' said Macleod, which caused Jona to look bizarrely at the screen. 'Too long a story,

Jona. Thank you both.'

Macleod closed down the call, stood up from his chair and walked over to the window. He felt like he should walk out into the office, stand around and catch a bit of chat with his colleagues, except they weren't there. He didn't want to go down to the canteen either. He had played his pieces and they were coming back with information. Now he needed Hope and Clarissa to come through with something. It seemed that the doctors were an important part of this puzzle. Everyone who died had been seeing one of them, but not the same one. What connection was there amongst them? Why were they important?

Macleod nearly jumped when his phone rang at the table, and he slowly turned before picking it up. 'Detective Inspector Seoras Macleod, how can I help?'

'This is Kiera Sedwell. I'm from the Minchlines ferry company, secretary to the CEO. He's asked me to advise you that we're having a lot of problems at the moment. We're getting mass cancellations.'

'I'm sorry to hear that,' said Macleod. 'I'm not quite sure how I can help.'

'He said you were in a meeting earlier on with him and he wanted you to be aware of the extent of the issues we're having because he didn't feel that you were taking him seriously enough in the meeting.'

Macleod thought back to the meeting. They were wittering on about passenger numbers, about people coming to the islands, and would the holiday season be okay. *There are people being killed*, Macleod had thought, *people dying. That's the key bit. That's the important bit. Not whatever tourist can or can't come*, and now the man had got his secretary to ring to reinforce the point.

Macleod wanted to pick up the phone, find the man, and throw it at him. How cheeky was that? Did he think Macleod had nothing to do except worry about his passenger numbers? About whether or not he was making a profit? Macleod had enough on his plate, but instead, he breathed in deeply and answered the woman politely.

'You can tell him that I'm very sorry for what's happening at the moment, but we are working earnestly to try and bring a killer to justice, and at this time, investigations are continuing.'

'He did ask me to get an update on how you were getting on, Detective Inspector.'

'The way we are getting on is that investigations are continuing. Tell him I thank him for his concern, but that frankly, at the moment, he needs to let us get on with our job. I'm sorry that you're having trouble with your passengers and if there's anything further, he can call directly to the Detective Chief Inspector, who I'm sure will be more than happy to answer any questions he has.'

'Thank you, Detective Inspector. I'll pass that on.'

Macleod thought he could hear in the woman's voice a little touch of sympathy for him, but he had none for the CEO. The DCI could handle him. That what was he was meant to do. Lift all of the minutiae off Macleod, let him get on with investigating.

He turned back to look at the laptop and thought about pressing it to try and communicate with Hope and Clarissa. He hated this time. He wanted answers and he wanted them now, but he had to wait for his pieces to play, to come through for him. What was he going to do in the meantime? Macleod wandered over to his door, opened it, and looked out into the main office. Maybe he'd teach some of these constables how to make proper coffee.

Chapter 17

larissa sat on the sofa in the hotel lobby, stretching her legs out in front of her. Opposite her in a chair was Hope McGrath, who scanned the people checking in.

'You can ease off, you know,' said Clarissa; 'you don't have to keep an eye on everybody in this entire building. Just relax until he gets here.'

'He's five minutes late,' said Hope.

'He's a doctor; of course, he's late. Probably could be anything up to half an hour to an hour. You know what they're like with appointments and that. They run over all the time.'

'That's not the point. He's meeting the police; you'd think he'd make an effort to arrive on time.'

'Still,' said Clarissa, 'gives us a chance to get a coffee. Have you spoken with anyone else?'

'I got a quick call down to Ross. He's just about wrapped up down in Islay, but he said that Dr Jacobs was also looking after Jenny Trimble and her husband, so we'll have a word about that while we're here. Makes sense. That's if he ever gets here.'

'Come on, wind down a bit. You've been up to high doh like anything.'

'No, I haven't. It's just . . . '

'You're becoming like Macleod; that's what it is.'

'What do you mean?'

'Seoras, when he's on the case, can't stop. It's all about the case, constantly. It's not me. I drop off at times, tune out for a bit, take a half hour here or there. Otherwise, it will drive you insane.'

'That's all right, but I'm the senior here. I'm the one who's meant to find things out.'

'There you go. That's taking Macleod's attitude. He's in charge, he's meant to solve everything, meant to get everything done. You can only do what you can do.'

'Well, sorry,' said Hope. 'I just can't take your "don't-give-a-stuff" attitude. I can't do that.'

'It's not a "don't-give-a-stuff" attitude. I just don't have time for piffle.'

'Piffle?' said Hope. 'Piffle is not a word I would associate with you.'

'No, but it's a reasonably posh hotel. I don't like saying other words.'

'I was born and raised in Glasgow; you can say whatever words you want. It's not like I haven't heard them before.'

'Well, piffle it is. A lot of time for piffle,' said Clarissa. 'You get the job and get stuck in, but sometimes when there's nothing left to do, you have to wait, chill out. Don't start marching around, getting up to high doh.'

Hope stood up, instantly began to walk, and then stopped and looked at Clarissa.

'That's what he does as well; he does that.'

'I am not becoming Macleod.'

'No, but in fairness, a lot of men wouldn't look at him the

way they look at you.' This drew a sharp look from Hope.

'What? Well, I'm sure Seoras has his admirers.'

'I'm sure he does,' said Clarissa, almost absentmindedly. Then glanced up to see Hope staring at her.

'Really?' said Hope. 'I thought you two were at loggerheads. It's not, is it? You're not? You're actually teasing him. You are, aren't you? You're teasing him with all that.'

'Well, he's a good man. A little bit stuck-up at times for my liking, but a good man.'

'You got him up to do karaoke. You had him singing things in front of the team, but you know his type, don't you? He's tight with Jane though.'

'I didn't say I wanted to marry him,' said Clarissa. 'All I said was he'd have his admirers.'

'Well, I've never heard you say that about anyone else,' said Hope. 'No one.'

'You've got to admit though, there is something about him.'

'Well, he'd probably have to be a good thirty years younger for me,' said Hope.

'That's so ageist,' said Clarissa. 'That's an ageist thing. Why can't he be thirty years older? Why can't the boy be thirty years younger than you?'

'Because then he'd be a child,' said Hope, 'if he was thirty years younger than me.'

'You know what I mean,' said Clarissa; 'it's only the age thing holding you back.'

'It's not just the age thing holding me back,' said Hope.

'Well, what else is there?' asked Clarissa.

Hope suddenly realised she was on the back foot for some reason. How did this happen? She'd gone after Clarissa having an interest in Macleod and now she was defending why she wasn't chasing the man.

'Well, he's my boss for a start.'

'I ask you for the reasons why you shouldn't be going after him and the best you can do is "He's my boss?" I thought I had it bad.'

Hope walked around the table and sat down beside Clarissa. 'You're lonely, aren't you?' she said.

'Yes,' said Clarissa, 'I am. Not many men will take me on. I'm too dynamic for them at this time of life, too hard to handle, especially now I'm older. When I was younger, men seemed to be more up for that, but not now. They want somebody quiet, somebody they can just curl up to at night, remind them where they left their keys.'

'Well, that's not you, is it?' said Hope.

'No. It's easy for you. Look at you, you and your car-hire man.'

'Don't bring John into this.'

'Why? I mean, what did he see in you?'

'Personality. My fun nature,' said Hope.

'I'm not saying he didn't, but what was the first thing he saw in you? Well, probably those legs for a start and that red hair.'

'Stop right there. He's not like that.'

'Of course, he's like that; he's a man.'

'Okay, he is like that,' said Hope, 'but he also appreciates the other sides of me.'

'And I'm not saying he doesn't,' said Clarissa, 'but looks fade. The longer you go on, the more you're reliant on your personality and if that's hard for them to handle, well, you end up like me, wedded instead to a green sports car.'

'He's still not here,' said Hope. 'I'm going to phone his secretary.'

'Okay,' said Clarissa. 'Good idea. It's better than walking up and down there, reminding me I don't have the legs you have.'

Hope stuck her tongue out at Clarissa, picked up her mobile, and called Dr Jacobs's office.

'Dr Jacobs's office; how can I help?'

'This is Detective Sergeant Hope McGrath. I was to meet with Dr Jacobs at his hotel tonight. Is he still there?'

'No. He left over an hour ago. He should be there by now. He said he was going to go back and get a shower before he met you.'

'Well, he's not arrived. Would you call him for me, find out what's happening?'

'Well, if anything's happened,' said the secretary, 'I think it's better if you ring him. I mean, you're a police officer after all, so I'll give you his mobile. I can trust you with that.'

Hope took the mobile number down.

'What's the matter?' asked Clarissa.

'Left an hour ago, still not here. I've got his mobile. Hang on,' said Hope. She dialled the number, but the phone just kept ringing.

'Wait a minute,' said Clarissa. She stood up and made her way over to reception. When she came back, she announced that room 235 was Dr Jacobs's. 'Let's go up and see what's happening,' said Clarissa, 'we can always ring from outside the room. See if it makes any sound.'

Together, the two women approached the lift, taking it to the second floor. Scanning the numbers on the doors, they walked down through a corridor before finding themselves in front of Dr Jacobs's room. Hope picked up the mobile and redialled the number. There was no answer from inside.

'I don't like this,' said Hope. 'Meant to be meeting us; we've got a murderer on the loose. I think we should check the room.'

'Do you really have cause to enter?' asked Clarissa.

'I've got the gut instinct that says I do. We'll not break in. We'll go down and ask the attendant at the lobby to come with us.'

'You stay here,' said Clarissa, 'I'll do that.' She disappeared off down the corridor and back to the lift.

Hope stood waiting, looking up and down the corridor to see if anyone approached. She rapped the door several times asking for Dr Jacobs, but there was no response. A door down the corridor opened and a couple came out wearing smart dress as if they were going out to dinner. They peered up as Hope banged the door and then the man marched along.

'It appears he doesn't want to be disturbed, whoever it is in there. I think you should go.'

'And who might you be?' asked Hope.

'I happen to be one of the local councillors so please don't take that attitude with me.'

Hope reached inside her jacket, took out her credentials, and held them up in front of the man. 'I'm a detective sergeant pursuing inquiries. Carry on to your night, please, sir.'

The man looked agitated, but he turned, made his way back down the hall, and started grumbling to his wife about what was going on. Hope resumed her banging on the door but got no answer. When Clarissa got back, she was accompanied by a woman who took a swipe card and passed it through the lock on the door of the room. Hope watched the little green light flash. She pushed down the handle and opened it gently.

'You better stay here,' said Clarissa, 'just in case there's anything untoward happening.'

The woman with the card nodded while Clarissa followed

Hope into the room. They could see a double bed stretched out with sheets that hadn't been pulled back. In the far corner there was a briefcase sitting on top of a small desk. It was opened. Clarissa took a look realising it had been rifled through. A jacket lay over a chair in the corner.

'He made it back here then,' said Hope, 'so where is he?'

Clarissa looked around the room, then marched over to the bathroom. She opened the door to see blood lying in large pools. Carefully, she stepped around it, reaching over to the bath that had a shower curtain pulled across it. With a gentle hand, she moved it back before it got caught midway. At this point, she could see a pair of hairy legs. Tilting her head so she could see the full extent of the bath, Clarissa took a deep breath inward. The man was lying there, blood all around him, his throat evidently slashed.

'We need to seal the room, Hope. Get Jona or one of her cronies down. It appears Dr Jacobs is in the bath.'

'In the bath?' queried Hope. She walked for the bathroom, but Clarissa held up a hand.

'No,' she said. 'Don't. It's not pretty.' She slowly made her way back out of the bathroom.

'You better phone Seoras with this,' said Clarissa. 'I'll deal with the staff member outside.'

Hope nodded, picked up her phone and dialled Macleod's number.

'Hope, it's about time. What have you learned?'

'I've learned that we're closer than we think,' said Hope. 'We saw Dr Stephens but we've moved on to Dr Jacobs.'

'Has Jacobs been of any use?' asked Macleod.

'No, he's dead. He's lying in a hotel bathroom with his throat slashed,' said Hope. 'Like I said, I think we're getting close,

Seoras.'

'What's your move then?'

'Well, we're going to seal off the room, obviously. We'll see if we can get forensics down. Take a look through the CCTV, if anybody came through.'

'No, Hope. I mean yes, but no. That's the basics. That's straightforward. What's your move now?'

'Well, I mean Dr Jacobs must have been important because there's two of the victims who had Dr Jacobs as their counsellor.

'But the others didn't,' said Macleod. 'You need to get hold of Dr Stephens and you need to get a hold of Dr Green.'

'You think they're in danger, too?' asked Hope. 'I mean we saw Stephens. We've already spoken to her.'

'But did she tell you everything? Whoever this is, clearly has been able to get information from the doctors. The important thing now to do is to make sure that they don't silence them or that link. Jacobs obviously knew of the person who's doing these killings. We have to assume that Stephens and Green will probably know them as well. We need to move. What's Clarissa doing?'

'She's out organising the hotel here. Shall I leave her to cover this off?'

'No. I wouldn't,' said Macleod. 'I'd send her for Green.'

'Why?' asked Hope. 'Surely it's better if I do it.'

'No. You'll guard him while being here because you'll learn more. You're a thorough detective. If Green's in trouble, Clarissa will haul him out of there, however she has to, and she'll haul in whatever force she needs to do it. Coordinate it. Don't do it all yourself.'

'Okay, Seoras, we'll get on it. I'll speak to you shortly.'

146

Clarissa came back into the room to a rather strange look from Hope. 'What's up?' she asked. 'I've just started to pull it together with the staff. They'll keep this room locked and marked off. She's gone off to get records and talk about where I can get CCTV.'

'You leave that to me,' said Hope. 'Got a job for you. Dr Green, find him. Put him somewhere safe.'

'Now you're talking,' said Clarissa.

Chapter 18

Hope had waved off Clarissa in her green sports car before returning to the hotel. A number of uniformed police had arrived, closing off the room, and a forensics section, at the request of Jona Nakamura, had made their way in from one of the Glasgow stations. Hope watched them go to it before taking aside the hotel staff one by one, asking if they'd seen anyone. She sat looking through CCTV as well, but she couldn't pin anyone to the room. There was CCTV in the lift, but no one had got in on that floor who couldn't be accounted for in the hotel. The hall that ran to Dr Jacobs's room had no CCTV. Hope interviewed everyone staying along it, but no one had seen anything.

Hope was in a bit of a fix, but she made sure she took images from the CCTV of everyone that was about the hotel. She sent them over to Ross who had used scanning software as well as his own eye in trying to see if anyone turned up at any of the murder sites more than once. Hope had tried ringing Dr Green's surgery, but got nowhere, and instead had rung his general practice. A constable assisted her, and after an hour and a half, they got hold of Doctor Green's home number. Although it rang, it was not answered. Neither was there any response from his mobile. Hope picked up her phone and called Clarissa who was racing up the A9 in her sports car.

'Where are you?'

'Pitlochry,' said Clarissa. 'I've got my foot down. What do you know?'

'Got his house number and his mobile. Not getting anything. Uniform popped round, but he wasn't in the house. However, I'd start there. If you're going to find anything, you're going to find it there.'

'Have uniform remained?'

'Negative. We don't know he's definitely in trouble, and they said they're not sitting there for the night. They've got plenty on.'

'That's fair enough. Where's Seoras at the moment?'

'He got called into a meeting. The ferries look like they're in trouble, cancellations left, right, and centre. They've got staff saying they're not going to work, thereby closing down all the ferries. It's a disaster for the islands.'

'Is that why the constables went round to the house and not Seoras himself?'

'Exactly,' said Hope. 'But I spoke to him, and he wanted you out there.'

'Well, I'm not that far off. I'll go direct to the house.'

'That's a good idea. He's stuck in this meeting, and he can't get out. He's not very happy with the new DCI, says he's hand-holding at the moment.'

'Well, I can see that would upset him. I'll be there shortly. I'll give you a call when I have something.'

Clarissa Urquhart closed the call and settled down for the drive through the night. She had pulled the hood up on her small sports car, the cool of the night too much to drive through, and she settled into a relaxed mode of driving. Many people wouldn't have recognised how calm she was for the car was hammering along. She hoped she wouldn't be stopped by anyone in a police car. It was always embarrassing when you had to explain you were hot-footing it to a potential crime scene.

Dr Green lived on the edge of Inverness. Clarissa drove up to the house, parking a short distance away before making her way slowly along the streets. She moved into the shadows but expected no one to be about at two o'clock in the morning.

She got closer. Clarissa stepped into the garden of a house across the street, scurried along behind some of their trees, and peered out towards the house of Dr Green. A light had gone on in an upstairs room. Clarissa wondered when he'd got back. She looked over and saw a car outside but had no idea whether it was his or not. Something caught her eye across the street and Clarissa froze.

There was a figure in the trees in the garden of Dr Green's house. She watched as the figure raised a camera and seemed to scan the lit window carefully. Clarissa crept back out of the garden into the street and edged her way along the opposite side in the shadows. When she got level with the person who was in Dr Green's garden, she stole quickly across the road, up on her tiptoes so her heels wouldn't make a sound.

As she got closer, Clarissa took a pair of handcuffs out from within her shawl, reached over the wall, and grabbed a man by the left arm, pulling it back hard. She heard a yell, and she slapped the cuffs on his wrist before grabbing his other arm and securing that wrist as well.

'Bloody hell. I'm just watching him, what's this?'

Clarissa recognised the voice. 'Well, it's been a while,' she said. 'What are you doing here?'

'Getting my arms taken off by the looks of it. Do you mind?' Clarissa grabbed the key for the cuffs and undid them as the man turned around to face her. 'I am here on legitimate business,' he said.

'Carl Mackenzie, I thought you'd given up with this sort of nonsense.'

'Not yet. I haven't got enough money stashed away. What about you? What are you doing here at two in the morning? I thought you were the high-classed, art-world detective. I see you more and more in the background of that Macleod guy. It's all a bit cut and thrust for you, isn't it?'

'I was always cut and thrust, darling,' said Clarissa, 'You just never got to find out.' Carl Mackenzie was a figure that Clarissa had run into many a time in her art dealings. If you wanted to know who was with whom, or who was cheating on whom, Carl was your man. He'd been hired by many of the richer clients simply because he was so good at exposing what their other halves were up to, but Clarissa thought he'd retired and finally got away with that package. It seemed he was still working.

'Who's hired you then?' asked Clarissa.

'My client, Mrs Green, has asked me to keep an eye on her husband, Dr Green, and a good job too.'

'What did you find out?'

'Not a lot. They came in from the rear, I think because I was out front so I don't know who's up there with him and I haven't got a photograph. I'm just going to wait until I see her emerge in the morning.'

'I'm sorry to do this to you Carl, but I'm about to go up and knock that door.'

'You can't. You can't do that,' he said.

'I'm afraid I can. Like you said, I now work for Macleod, and this is a murder investigation I'm on. It can't wait for your paycheque.'

'Well, that's just charming,' he said. 'We've all got to make a living, you know that?'

'When did they come?'

'Less than an hour,' he said. 'I got a call from my client; she said somebody had been ringing, couldn't find her husband.'

'Well then, looks like I'm responsible for your fee. That's us checking up on him.'

'Checking up him? Why? Is there something afoot? I'm not in a dangerous situation, am I?'

The man was sitting in a hedge, trying to expose another man for cheating on his wife, and Clarissa was wondering just how dangerous the situation needed to get. People under that sort of duress, especially when exposed, didn't tend to hold back.

'No, you'll be all right here,' she said. 'But I'm going up to that door. I will suggest that you go around the rear and you might be able to catch some good photographs, but I start walking in fifteen seconds.'

'You ever regret it?' said Carl, starting to walk away.

'The time you propositioned me?' said Clarissa. 'No, I don't regret it.'

'I do. Everyday. Just saying, if retirement gets lonely.'

And with that, the man was gone. Clarissa shook her head. She was lonely. She had told Hope as much, but she wasn't that lonely.

Clarissa turned and marched across the garden, up a set of stone steps to a large wooden door. There was a brass knocker and a bell, but Clarissa took the knocker and started slamming it like it needed to wake the hounds of hell. She continued for the next three minutes until a man opened the door dressed in his dressing gown, bare legs beneath it.

'What the blazes are you doing?' he said.

'Are you Doctor Green?' asked Clarissa.

'Yes, I'm Dr Green. What the hell do you want?'

'I want to come in and make sure you're okay. My name's Detective Sergeant Clarissa Urquhart, and we have been contacting you because we've been worried about your safety. Firstly, you've neither picked up the house phone nor the mobile so here I am knocking. It's a good job you answered. I'd have been forced to kick in the door. Do you mind if I come in?'

'Of course, I bloody mind if you come in; it's two in the morning.'

'You look rather out of breath,' said Clarissa. 'Is anyone else in the house?'

The man looked over his shoulder, 'No. Nobody.'

'You won't mind if I come in then? I just want to check around. I believe that your life may be in danger.'

'My life in danger? Why?'

'I take it you know a Dr Jacobs, works out of Aberdeen, similar line of work to yourself.'

'Of course, I do. It's not that big a community amongst us.'

'Found dead tonight, throat slit. May have a possible link to the murder investigation that we're looking into, one that has your name in it.'

'My name in it? What do you mean?'

'Yes, a link to clients you have. A number of them have died. I'm just going to check upstairs if you don't mind.'

Clarissa could hear something, somebody upstairs, but she didn't let on. Instead, she marched up, and spotted the main bedroom and walked into it. The main bed sheets were a mess, and Clarissa sniffed the air. There was a heavy musk perfume.

'I'm going to need you to come with me to the station,' said Clarissa. 'I'm sorry about the late hour, but it needs to be done.'

'Dead?' said the man. 'Jacobs is dead?'

'Very much so,' said Clarissa. 'I believe that could be quite upsetting for you, but that's the way it is. Please, go and get changed.'

'I'm going to have a shower first,' he said. 'Is that okay?'

'By all means,' said Clarissa.

She stood in the bedroom until she heard the man lock the bathroom door. She went over to where a range of perfumes sat on the dresser, checking out each one. They were women's perfume, but none of them actually matched the scent that was in the air. When she heard the shower still continuing, she made her way downstairs and out to the rear door of the house, stepping outside and letting the light flood into the garden. She gave a wave and Carl Mackenzie emerged from the bushes.

'Did you see anyone come out?' asked Clarissa.

'Yes,' he said and turned his camera around so she could see the LCD screen at the rear of it. There was a woman who looked like she'd been dressed in a hurry, clutching a number of bags, exiting the rear of the house.

'Do you know her?' asked Clarissa.

'Well, yes, I do. Apparently, she's a friend of Mrs Green. Close friend in fact. Very naughty, but I think I've got her banged to the rights, and him as well.'

'Hang on to it for a couple of days,' said Clarissa.

'Why?' asked Carl. 'I've done my job.'

'Indeed, but he's going to be in interview with us for a little while. Probably best to deliver the goods when his wife will have a little bit less in sympathy with him. Might get you a bigger fee.'

'That's what I liked about you,' said Carl. 'You can always see past what is going on.'

'Well, the sooner you get a bigger fee, the sooner you retire,' said Clarissa. 'And the sooner you realise that retirement without me is perfectly fine.' Carl smiled and turned away, giving Clarissa a wave.

'Text me that picture,' said Clarissa. 'I just need to make sure she's not in our inquiry.'

'And if she is?'

'That camera's coming in for evidence.'

'Well then, I hope she isn't.'

Clarissa walked back inside, and on returning upstairs, she could hear that the shower had finished. She knocked the bedroom door and Dr Green asked her to wait for a moment while he was still getting changed. She heard a beep on her phone and looked at the image that had arrived from Carl Mackenzie. It wasn't that clear. She blew it up on the phone as much as she dared and then started walking around the house, looking for photographs of friends of Doctor Green's wife. There were a number here and there of different charity functions or dinners they'd been to. Clarissa compared each one. Well, Mackenzie must have been wrong. There was no close friend here. Nobody that matched the image she was looking at.

Dr Green came out of his room. 'Are we ready?' he said. 'Let's go and get this done.'

'You sure there was no one here tonight?'

'No,' said Dr Green. 'My wife's away, you see. On my own.'

Clarissa let the statement slide for a moment. She'd take him into the interview room and soon sort him out, because the guy was lying through his teeth.

Chapter 19

Hope stood behind two constables in a Glasgow police station looking at the CCTV video footage in front of her. They had reviewed nearly all of it and interestingly, the two constables in front of her believed they'd narrowed down a certain suspect.

'If you look here, Sergeant, she comes through, hangs around in the lobby for a bit, then disappears back out. She's back in again, comes upstairs, then disappears downstairs. Here, Dr Jacobs comes in. This is after she's gone outside again, but this time when she comes in, she once again ends up taking the lift up to Dr Jacobs's floor, and she gets out. Ten minutes later, she gets back in again. She comes downstairs and disappears into the night.'

'Pause it on her,' said Hope. The woman before her never looked up at the camera once but she had red hair like Hope and a large pair of dark sunglasses on. The image was quite grainy, and Hope found it difficult to work out exactly what the woman looked like.

'I thought these CCTV cameras had gotten better these days.'

'It was quite an old one in that lift though,' said the constable. 'I agree with you; it's a bit of a disappointing image considering how long she was up there.'

'It doesn't prove anything either. It could have been some-body in the hall. Came and did it and then went back to their room. We'll need to have a look through though. Can you send that image off to Detective Constable Ross? He's got images from everywhere else. He might be able to connect that image too. See if that woman was at any of the other murders.'

'Will do,' said the constable.

Hope thanked them for their time, and she made her way down to the canteen within the station house, realising it was four o'clock in the morning. Her eyes were almost closing but she knew she'd need to take a run-out again to the hotel just to check off that everything was closed off. She'd take an image of the woman as well, put it in front of the guests, see if anybody recognised her, or could give a better description. That would require taking more of the constables with her, the last job of the night shift before they went home.

Hope sat and looked into her coffee. She was a little bit off just now. That was the way to describe it. She was out here working on her own, something she'd done before but she felt a little bit blindsided that Macleod said to send Clarissa all the way back up to Inverness. She wasn't sure how to read it. Did he not trust her to get that job done? Was she too precious to go? What did he mean by it? Or did he simply want everything done right in Glasgow, so he needed her there?

The team was spread very thin at the moment, and it had been a long time since a case had them travelling so far. Most murders occurred fairly close to the other in a particular series, especially when committed by the same person, but this killer had travelled quite happily, setting things up on different ferries. Were they trying to disguise it? Did they actually hope

158

to get away with it? Clearly, the efforts of the investigation team had spooked them. For whoever it was, she had come, as Hope believed, to finish Dr Jacobs off.

Hope smelled the chips that were just being poured into a large canteen tray and she succumbed, standing up, and strode over to pick up a plateful. She sat down with them, ate about half of them, and then felt that she really couldn't finish that sort of food at this time of night. She picked up her phone and called through to John, her partner in Inverness, the car-hire man.

'What time is it? What's happened?' he said quickly on answering the phone.

'Nothing's happened, I just wanted to talk.'

'About what? You're not pregnant, are you?'

'No, I'm not pregnant, I don't need to talk about that. I'm just . . . , well, I don't know what.'

'Are you all right? I can come down if you want.'

'That's not going to work,' said Hope; 'we're at the tail end of this investigation, and frankly, I'm probably going to be back up in Inverness soon. It's just been an awkward one—it really has. I'm down on my own away from the team. Ross is over at Oban, Clarissa was with me but raced up to Inverness. Macleod's stuck in meetings all the time. It's just weird; we've never worked this far apart before. I haven't even seen Jona.'

'Why, where's she?'

'Last I heard, she was down with Ross, following the dead bodies around. I've had to work with the local force. They're fine, it's just it's not our guys, it's five in the morning, and I'm just sick of this at the moment.'

'Is there anything you want me to do?' asked John.

'I want you to make it all go away,' said Hope, 'I want to be back up there.'

'You sound like you're having problems,' said John. 'Are you okay? It's not us, is it?'

'No, it's not us; it's nothing to do with you. I'm not blaming you for anything.' Hope stopped instead of going on with the sentence. *That's it*, she thought. *It's blame. It's all blame; she's blaming them. It's always this side, the partner who's caused the issue, killing the cause of the problem.*

'Thanks, John, that's great, but I've got to go.'

'You called me,' he said, 'I'm not going to go back to sleep now, the least you can do is talk to me.'

'Sorry, I need to phone Seoras.'

Hope cut John off and immediately dialled Macleod's number. When he picked it up, she could hear the foul mood he was in.

'I've literally stepped out. I need the bathroom. What?'

'Sorry, I'm stuck down here in Glasgow at five in the morning as well, you know, but I got something.'

'What?' asked Macleod.

'This person, who's doing this, I think they've been shunned by their partner. I think they've been put off. Something has happened to them, they've been in counselling or something, or they've seen it up close. They're blaming the person who has done the most damage in the relationship; don't you see it?

'Andrew Culshaw, he's violent. Peter Hughes was pushing Gerald Lyndhurst to come out about their relationship. Daphne Walsh was a wild woman, Fred Martin, he was the one that caused his wife's problems, why she committed suicide. The murderer has blamed him. That's why he's dead even though she's already jumped. Then you have Jenny Trimble;

she's been running around on her husband. He's played the good guy, not getting divorced, but she hasn't. She's been the one causing the problems. Therefore, the murderer's gone for her.'

'Okay,' said Macleod, 'but what's the ferry bit?'

'I think they've thought that they can get away with it by making it look like suicide. Also, I think it's a woman. We've got a potential female who's in and around Dr Jacobs's room when he dies. Trouble is the CCTV's so poor. I'm going to have to go back out and canvass everyone in the hotel and see if I can get a better description of her. She's gone to the ferry source because, think about it, you can kill them, and they disappear below the sea. I think she's reckoning on them not being picked up or turning up so late that anyone looking won't see her as a part of it.'

'Needs to be a certain somebody though,' said Macleod, 'who knows how to use Ketamine. What about all these doctors? They're good for it, aren't they?'

'Well, it wasn't Dr Jacobs,' said Hope; 'he's dead.'

'They all know each other, don't they? In that sort of a field, maybe they talk about issues, maybe they talk about clients. Maybe that's what's done it. What do you think about that? I think it could be one of these doctors. Clarissa's holding Dr Green. He's coming in at the moment and I'm going to sit and interview him; see what I can extract from him.'

'Could be the other way around, of course; could be the partners. Who do you talk about at home, about the work, and what's going on, your partner?'

'I don't,' said Macleod, 'I talk to you about that. I only talk to Jane about how I'm feeling. She doesn't want to know about the other side, says it's too grim.'

'Yes, but we're police officers. Other people on normal jobs, it's a bit less gruesome. People love to talk about what they're doing, especially if they've got problems. Maybe we should be checking out the wives of these doctors or the partners.'

'That's a good idea. See if they can get photos of their partners. You can get a better ID, either through CCTV or with the people in the hotel, see if we can pull this together. I take it you sent the image off to Ross.'

'Hopefully, he'll be looking at it. We'll be lucky to get a match though due to the grainy quality. To be honest, I think it's a long shot at the moment, Seoras. We're going to need to get hold of him. Whittle this down. There's something that these doctors know. Somebody's got to be able to break this open.'

'Well, I hope we do soon because I've just had it in the neck from the ferry company, from the politicians, from the rather useless DCI. I'm only saying that to you. I'm sick of sitting in a room and telling them we're getting on with it and not being allowed to get on with it because I'm sat in a stupid room with them.'

Hope could feel the rage coming from Macleod. 'Easy, Seoras. Easy. We'll get this. You'll get it. You always do.'

'We'll get it. I'm just frustrated. I've been waiting for all the pieces to come to place. I've sent you all out, you've all done your jobs, and it's not there yet. Why? What are we not seeing? Who are we not seeing?'

'Maybe we don't know them yet.'

'Then we need to get to know these people.'

'Do you want me up the road tomorrow?' asked Hope. 'We can pool resources that way.'

'No,' said Macleod, 'you've got Dr Stevens down in Glasgow, Jacobs was Aberdeen, Green is up here in Inverness. I want you down there. The Glasgow contingent are good, but I need somebody from our team there to organise and supervise. You carry the rank of authority outside of me. Clarissa will only upset people. I hate to say it, but I think sometimes she needs a handler with her.'

'Well, you can tell her that,' said Hope, 'because there's no way I am. Is that why I was down here with her?'

'Well, since she came in, look at the things she's gotten into. Absolutely, you were down there to oversee it, look after, make sure nothing went crazy. She's great for tearing a place up, but you can't leave the carnage behind.'

Hope thought of what Clarissa had said about Macleod and wondered what she'd make of him saying that she was too forward, too much chaos, and not enough of the steely but controlled attitude that a detective needed to have.

'I better get organised,' said Hope, 'get back out there and interview these guests again.'

'Go at them but be gentle. It's five o'clock in the morning. We're not at our best at five in the morning.'

'Well, I'm not,' said Hope, 'I'm not my best at all.'

She closed the phone call down and thought of John before picking up the phone again and dialling John's number.

It rang eight times before a blurry answer went, 'What now?'

'Sorry, I just phoned up to apologise.'

'I just got off to sleep,' said John.

'Sorry,' said Hope, 'I don't know when I'm coming back up. Seoras has me staying down this end. Are you all right?'

'I'm fine,' said John, 'I could honestly just do with my sleep, but if you need me . . .'

'No,' said Hope, 'it's fine. You go to sleep.'

She never thought she would lie to him, but she needed him

right there and then to sit and listen, and yet, she didn't even know why. What was up with her of late?

Hope closed the call and made her way up towards the offices at the top end of the Glasgow station. There she would find the constables that she'd take with her to start interviewing more of the hotel guests. She'd print out an image, see if anyone had seen this woman, and what she'd done.

As Hope looked out of the window, the printer sending out multiple copies of the woman's face, Hope saw the red sun starting to come up against the city skyline. She realised what was up. This had been home. This had been where she'd grown up. Yet here she was working with Glasgow's finest, operating in and out of the city that had been such a part of her and right now, it felt as far away from home as it could possibly get.

Chapter 20

Macleod stretched in his office chair, trying to push away the sore bones and shoulders that were currently causing him pain at this early hour of the morning. Clarissa was sitting across from him at the small table they used for conference and he could see her eyes beginning to droop.

'Come on, up and at it.'

'Seoras, when you signed up, what age did you think you'd still be doing this kind of shift?'

'I never thought about it,' said Macleod, 'I didn't back then, then after the wife died, any time of day was fine. I can see now though, it affects Jane.'

'It affects me,' said Clarissa. 'If I don't get my head down on a good bed, when I get up, I'm achy; everything just feels off.'

'And you get grumpy,' said Macleod.

Clarissa looked up quickly, a shocked look on her face. 'I get grumpy? I'm not the obsessive one, I'm not the one that . . .'

'Can we just get on?' said Macleod. 'What is this with you? Every time I say a comment about you, you fire it back at me. I never thought I'd get to this age and somebody of a similar age would be sitting fighting the bit all the time.'

'Don't you age bit that on me,' said Clarissa.

'You were the one who was just starting to say about it,' said Macleod.

'I'm allowed to, just you remember. I'm a lady; you speak nicely.'

Macleod raised his eyebrows then pointed to the door. As Clarissa walked to it, Macleod strode round from behind her and pulled the door open.

'For the lady,' he said. She stuck her tongue out at him.

The pair walked in silence down two flights of stairs into an interview room in Inverness Police Station. Inside was Dr Green, who was looking a little bedraggled and also extremely tired. Macleod pulled a seat out for Clarissa, who sat down giving him a glare. Macleod then joined her on the seat beside and put his hands together on the table looking across at Dr Green. The man raised his head, his eyes were starting to well up. Macleod pitched him as maybe middle-aged, and he could tell a face of regret as soon as he saw one.

'I'm Detective Inspector Seoras Macleod; you've already met Detective Sergeant Clarissa Urquhart. We're going to ask you some questions about tonight. More specifically about this woman.'

Macleod took an envelope that was on the table and pulled out a sketchy image of the woman who had left Dr Green's house.

'That's Janine, Inspector. I'm having an affair with her.'

'Well, that's pretty straightforward. Janine who?'

'I don't know.'

'Well, how did you meet her then?'

'She was at a hotel down in Glasgow. I was in the bar; I remember it was quite late. She came up to me and she was

166

wearing this rather knock-out dress. The missus had given me a hard time, has been for the last lot of years, and well, Janine was so attentive. Pretty soon we ended up talking until the small hours of the morning. She suggested that we go back up to my room, with a bottle of red. It all kind of went from there.'

'I can understand the one off,' said Clarissa, 'but it went from there. Who suggested it went from there?'

'Well, we both found out that actually, we live up round the Inverness area, so Janine said, "Why don't we do this again?" She said she enjoyed it; it was good. Told me how good I was. I said, "Yes," but obviously, we needed somewhere to go and if we were in Inverness, we couldn't kind of do it in the hotels around there. Too easy to get caught out, seen by people. Seen by my clients, even.'

'True,' said Macleod, 'so where did you go for your quiet times?'

The man bent his head forward. Macleod saw the tears coming from his eyes.

'I didn't mean to do it. Well, it wasn't my fault. It's just, she was so available, and she treated me nice. She treated me well. She built me up. My wife she just takes. Do you know what that's like? Just takes and . . .'

There came a loud sobbing from the man and Macleod sat back for a moment, giving him time to let the emotion flow through. It wasn't the time to press him. He'd speak wildly. Better to let him regain his composure. Macleod wanted accurate facts, not some hysterical nonsense. He looked over at the constable sat in the room and called him across.

'Get me a coffee, please,' he said. 'Don't go to the machine either; up to the team office, bring one down. Clarissa here

167

will have one as well. Dr Green, do you want anything? Can we get you a cup of water, coffee, tea? Give you a moment to steady yourself.'

But the man just simply cried. Macleod waited five minutes until the coffee had returned and the constable was dismissed to stand outside the room.

'So, Janine,' said Macleod breaking the still-whimpering sobs of Dr Green. 'Janine built you up, so where did you go for your quiet moments?'

The man raised his eyes. 'I could only know of one place we could truly be safe. Well, we suggested her place, but she said no, the neighbours were too close and nosey, so she suggested that we do it at the surgery where I carry out my work.

'Okay,' said Macleod, 'and how often?'

'Two to three times a week. Occasionally, she was going away though, but when she was about, it was two to three times a week.'

'And what? A quick hour in the afternoon. How did you work it?'

'Oh, no, at night. Always at night. We slept there. I'd tell the wife I was off with a client, or I was working late, had to stay over at a hotel. She seemed to buy it, so we managed to spend the night together. Always a bottle of red. That was Janine, always a bottle of red. I can't take a bottle of red, you see. Too many glasses and after a bit of exertion, I'd fall asleep, and that'd be me until morning.'

Macleod shot a glance at Clarissa; he could see she was thinking the same thing. Dr Green was paralytic, fast asleep. The woman could gain access to any of the records in his office.

'So, you're telling me,' said Macleod, 'that you took this woman to your office, you had sex with her, drank a lot of

168

wine, you would pass out and then in the morning, you'd just get on with it or head off to wherever?'

'We were gone by six. My secretary sometimes comes in at eight, sometimes even earlier so we were well clear.'

'And you hold all your records there, do you?'

'My records, my notes, everything,' he said. 'Why?'

'Inside your office, are they locked away?'

'Well, we have the filing system for the handwritten notes and that. They do go on the computer, but they don't get locked away in the cabinet. The cabinet is usually open; there's no point. I lock the office door.'

'Just to confirm,' said Clarissa, 'you're saying to me that you slept in this office. You were then out for the count and this woman could have had access to any of the documents there. Would you have known? Would you have heard her move to get them?'

Green suddenly sat up and stared across the table. 'No, I wouldn't. Why? Why are you asking me about my records?'

'Have you read the news recently? I'm thinking particularly about Peter Hughes.'

'Peter? Yes, I heard the tragic story—fell off the ferry.'

'No,' said Clarissa, 'we believe he may have been murdered and dumped off the ferry, and we believe it may have been because he was trying to force Gerald Lyndhurst to come out in a relationship.'

'How did you know about that?'

'Well, Gerald told me, and we believe somebody else knew about it, and we believe it came from your office.'

The man froze and stared. 'How do you mean?'

'We believe that someone has been targeting couples that have been having problems, but especially that person in their

169

relationship that was causing the problem.'

'Peter Hughes was the problem,' said Dr Green. 'He really was; he wanted to force Gerald into coming out. He had an obsession about everyone knowing. An obsession about being clean that came from his childhood when he had to repress everything, but that was all in the notes. I mean they were my private notes where I said that, the ones that were held . . . oh dear God. Really?'

'What did you tell this Janine woman?' asked Macleod.

'How do you mean?'

'What did you tell her about your clients?'

'Nothing. Nothing. I mean, usually when we talked it would have been about me, about . . . '

'Your wife?' suggested Clarissa.

'Yes, it would have been my wife and what she was doing with me in the relationship and how it was hard because she never cared, and she always forced me to the . . . , you don't . . . '

'Where is your wife?' asked Macleod.

'She's away; she's on holiday; took a trip with a lot of her friends. She's down in England.'

'Have you got the name of the hotel?' asked Macleod.

'I do. I do. You don't think . . . '

'I don't think she's in trouble tonight,' said Macleod. 'Janine was with you. To be honest, I think at the moment you may be in trouble, because Dr Jacobs got killed for what he knew. We believe that he may have been infiltrated somehow but hid the information about his clients. Although we're not sure how yet.'

'But she was there tonight.'

'Yes, she was,' said Macleod; 'describe her to us.'

'Well, Janine's in her thirties, at least that's what she said. She's got dark brown hair. She's strong for her size. Maybe about five feet seven, can handle herself. Very energetic, but she came tonight, and she didn't kill me. We were going through our usual routine. I was surprised because she came to the house. I didn't care because the wife's away, so I thought, why not? In fact, I was quite interested to take her to the bed. That would show my wife, wouldn't it? Have somebody else in there. Oh, dear God. What did I do? She could've . . . '

'I think if Sergeant Urquhart hadn't arrived, we may have found you dead in the morning,' said Macleod. 'I don't think you'll be going anywhere quickly. I'm going to advise the local constabulary where your wife is and get an interview with her about what's going on.'

'You can't tell her. You can't tell her; she'll go crazy.'

'I think that bird's flown,' said Clarissa. 'We're in the middle of a murder investigation and we think that the murderer may even have been with you tonight. You were intimate with her. This is not a patch-up job. You need to understand, Dr Green, these things are going to come out at some point.'

The man put his head in his hands and began weeping again on the table.

'I'll be sending along a sketch artist. I want you to tell him exactly what Janine looked like so we can get a sensible image up, see if we can find out who she really is,' said Macleod. 'You can stay here at the station for a while. It's probably safest until we work out where Janine is.'

With that parting shot, he stood up, draining what remained of his coffee and walking out to the corridor outside. Clarissa followed him. Once the door was shut, Macleod turned round to her. 'Blast,' he said, 'she was there. Whoever she is, she was

171

there.'

'But we can get a decent image now. If we get the sketch artist, we'll soon find out what she looks like and then we'll need to get that image in front of the rest of our medical professionals. Well, Stephens, at least. See if she knows who it is. Because that's the weird one, isn't it? She's clearly going to bed with Dr Green. Dr Jacobs, well, we'll see, but she got into his room. But I'm not sure about Dr Stephens. She may have played a fast one there, coming from a different angle.'

'We'll wait and see,' said Macleod. 'Modern age, you don't know who's doing what with who. I've learnt to have a much more open mind these days.'

'I stand corrected,' said Clarissa, beginning to walk back up to the office. 'Modern Macleod has told me so.'

Chapter 21

Alan Ross had driven through the night, and the morning sun felt sore on his eyes. He had the windows rolled down, trying to make himself feel better, but in truth, he was tired. Dr Jacobs's surgery in Aberdeen was right in the heart of the city, and as Ross drove through the early morning traffic, he found himself having to concentrate harder due to the sheer volume of cars on the road. He'd come up through the night when hardly anyone was about, and although he struggled to see much due to the darkness, it had been, up until Aberdeen, a very pleasant drive.

It had been a while since he'd been out on his own. He was always with Macleod or Clarissa, or even Hope. In some ways, he thought Macleod was too protective of him after that time in the Monarch Isles. It wasn't Macleod's fault he got shot, and in fact, he'd only been shot after everyone else had arrived. He always thought he had coped admirably with the situation until others had joined in, trying to round up the drug dealers.

Ross parked the car in a large multi-storey car park, took the lift down because his legs were feeling so tired, and then walked across the centre of the city until he saw a set of serviced offices high up. Ross looked up the list alongside the main door before buzzing and asking for Dr Jacobs's office.

'This is Dr Jacobs's office. I'm afraid he's not here yet. Do you have an appointment?'

'I'm Detective Constable Alan Ross. I'd like to come up and speak to you if that's okay, madam?'

'Absolutely. Of course,' she said. 'I'll just buzz you in. We're up here on the fifth floor.'

Ross pushed open the glass door in front of him, again walked over to a lift and stood in silence as he was transported up to the fifth floor. He closed his eyes due to the brightness inside, but when he heard the ping and the doors begin to open, he gave out a large yawn, flicked his eyes several times to try and take any remaining sleep out of them. He told himself to get his brain into gear for, after the long drive, the business end of his trip had arrived.

A set of large double doors had the motif for Dr Jacobs's surgery on them, and Ross gave a quick knock before opening one of them and stepping inside. A secretary was sitting behind a desk tapping away on her computer but stood up on seeing him and walked out from behind the desk. Ross thought she was older than he, dressed in a rather neat skirt, blouse and jacket, looking like the perfect professional's assistant.

'I'm sorry to bother you. I'm Detective Alan Ross,' he said, pulling out his credentials. 'When was the last time you saw Dr Jacobs?'

'Oh, that would have been two days ago, although I did speak to him yesterday during the day. I had to send him down some information on some clients. He's down in Glasgow at the moment doing some work. He'll be back up later today.'

'If you take a seat, madam. What's your name?'

'Mrs Thompson,' said the woman, starting to look concerned.

'Is there anything wrong?' she asked.

'I'm afraid there is, Mrs Thompson; your employer was unfortunately killed last night in his hotel in Glasgow.'

Her hand flew up to her mouth and the words 'Dear God' arrived.

'How? What do you mean killed? Was he in an accident or something?'

'No. I'm afraid he was murdered,' said Ross, 'in his hotel room. I need to ask you some questions.'

'I was up here. I was at home with my husband.'

'I'm not saying you're in the frame for anything, so please calm down and don't worry. What I do need to know is a little bit about Dr Jacobs and what's been going on in his day-to-day work.'

The woman looked away from Ross for a moment, but he could see her shoulders begin to shake. Then she seemed to turn round resolutely to him. 'I'll get you some coffee,' she said. 'Yes, you've come in, you should be getting coffee. I'll do that now. Take a seat. I'll tend to you now.'

'No,' said Ross. 'You've clearly had a shock. Sit there. I see the coffee and tea and things over there, I'll get you something. I think you need a cup of tea. It's clearly been a shock for you.'

The woman said nothing but simply stared over at the wall.

Ross made some tea with a lot of sugar in it and a hefty dose of milk before taking it back to the woman. He watched as she sipped it and he encouraged her to drink more of it until he saw the cup go down on the table. Ross pulled a chair around it and sat directly opposite her.

'Mrs Thompson, I need you to try to think clearly, if you can do that for me. Dr Jacobs, in recent weeks or even months, has there been anything different about him? Any trouble with his wife?'

'She's dead. He's a widower. Has been for a number of years. He needs a little bit of looking after in that respect. You go above and beyond as a secretary.'

'In what way?' asked Ross.

'Sorting him out with ties; sometimes you have to go and make sure he's got new shirts and things, organise that for him. He comes in with trousers and they're the wrong size. They're not right and you have to go and get them altered. He just . . . , well, he clearly missed someone who could look after certain sides of his life.'

'The other sides of his life, was there any change in them?'

'In what way do you mean?' asked Mrs Thompson.

'Well, he obviously lost a partner when his wife died, so has anyone come in to replace her?'

'I'm not one to gossip about my employer. I wouldn't want him to find out.' She then stopped. 'He's not going to find out, is he?' Tears rolled down off her cheeks, but Ross tried to keep her talking.

'You said you wouldn't speak out of turn; there's no out of turn anymore. He's been murdered. I need to know if anything was different, unusual.'

'She was. The client, Kerry Watson. I knew there was something about her. He said she had some sort of trauma that he was trying to work through. She would come in here always with a scarf over her head, although her blonde hair rolled out behind, sunglasses too, but she dressed that way. When you're a woman, you know how other women are dressing. You can tell when they're fishing for something or trying to entice. She wasn't incredibly overt with what she was doing, but she was trying to trap him in. Dr Jacobs had lost his wife, so I didn't feel it was my place to comment. She was taking advantage of him clearly.'

'In what way?' asked Ross.

The woman almost looked embarrassed. 'In that way,' she said.

'Sexually?' asked Ross for clarification.

'Yes.'

'How do you know that?' asked Ross.

'Well, she would come in here—it'd be the morning or the afternoon—into his office; the door would get locked and well, you hear things, don't you? You know what I mean? They'd be out of breath. You'd go in afterwards and you could tell people had been energetic in that room.'

The woman was clearly having difficulty with what she was saying and trying to put it in a fashion that didn't make it sound sordid.

'This Kerry Watson, did you ever see any ID, or . . . '

'None. Dr Jacobs said just let her come and go. She never paid anything either.'

'Do you know if he saw her outside of this office?'

'No. I don't know. I do know that they did row about it once. I wasn't listening, I was just sitting here at my desk, and I remember her saying that because of her husband, she couldn't. Said she'd been married, or was married, and she couldn't go elsewhere, it would have to be in the office, always in the office.'

'How long were these meetings?'

'Well, quite often they'd go on over lunch. I remember because Dr Jacobs used to come out and you'd look at him and you'd think, 'Yes, you've tried to dress yourself again quickly in a hurry.' He'd pop out to the off-license and next day there would be empty bottles of champagne.

'He never sent me for the booze. Never, which I found a little bit odd, but maybe he just wanted to keep all that to himself. He was a widower at the end of the day. Not my place to interfere in his personal affairs. If it affected his business I might have said, but if he wanted to spend two or three hours in there with that woman, that's his business. My job was to man the phones and organise his appointments and his work. I'm not here to deal with his private life.'

'I understand,' said Ross; 'there's no need to blame yourself.'

'Do you think that she was the one that did it then? Do you think she killed him down in Glasgow?'

'We don't know,' said Ross, 'but can you give me a better description of what she looked like?'

'No, I can't,' said Mrs Thompson. 'I really can't. She came in either with a headscarf on or a hood of some sort. She'd always have big sunglasses on, the kind you can't see through as well. As I say, it was blonde hair because I saw that straggling out the back of the hood at times, but outside of that, smallish lips, sort of a roundish nose, but very hard to tell you. Her ears I never saw.

'What about her height?' asked Ross. 'How tall was she?'

'Oh, maybe five feet seven, maybe five feet eight. I say that because I'm five feet seven and she was round about my height.'

'Anything else you can tell me about her?'

'Well, she wasn't married.'

'Why do you say that?' asked Ross.

'There was one time she came in and whatever had happened, she had got something on her hand. It was like jelly or something and she had to get it off the ring she was wearing but she came out to me still in sunglasses and the scarf, and she took the ring off to give it a wipe and clean it up. There was no mark underneath. Look.'

Mrs Thompson took her hand and put it in front of Ross. She removed her wedding ring and he stared down.

'You see the mark? Clearly, I wear a ring right there. When that Kerry Watson came in, there was nothing underneath, but I thought maybe she was trying to take him for a ride, look after his money, but then she was coming on with the marriage story, so I didn't know what she was after. He seemed to be enjoying himself; that's why I didn't interfere. That's why I didn't. You don't think I should have, do you?'

'No,' said Ross. 'You were being what you should've been, a good secretary. I'm very sorry for your loss. I'm going to have a sketch artist come along. I want you to try and remember as best you can what Mrs Watson looked like. I don't suppose there's any CCTV is there?

'You can try the building. They might have some, but we don't have any access to that. There's none in the office. There's no way they would've got up to what they got up to with that in the office.'

'I guess not,' said Ross. 'Can I call anyone for you? You're obviously in quite a distressed state.'

'Let me call my husband,' she said. 'If you'd stay with me until he comes.'

It was half an hour later when Ross left the building. Mrs Thompson's husband had arrived as well as a sketch artist, and Ross left them to it. He picked up the phone calling Macleod but found him unavailable as he'd been pulled in with the DCI again. Clarissa Urquhart answered, however.

'From what you're telling me, this looks like the same person. I'll get hold of Hope.'

179

'The thing I don't get,' said Ross, 'is how do we get hold of this person, where they're at? We might have a face, but if it doesn't hold up on any records, how do we go after them? Where do we tail them to? Are we simply hanging around people until she comes to kill them because they know too much? Who's to say there won't be more occurrences on the ferries.'

'Well, they won't be happening for a while. They cancelled the ferries today.'

'That's not good,' said Ross. 'The boss is going to be angry at that one.'

'You better believe it. He's in his office next door on the phone. You should have heard him shout when they announced it.'

Chapter 22

What do you mean find me someone? I can't just find you someone. This is a murder investigation. You have to work your way through; we have to collect evidence. You don't just haul somebody out for it.'

Clarissa watched Macleod slam the phone down on his desk and then sit back in his chair. He was staring up at the ceiling, but his face was red with rage. Despite this, she marched up to the door, knocked it loudly, and opened it without waiting for a 'Come in.'

'Got information for you.'

'Good,' said Macleod, 'shut the door.' Clarissa turned round and closed the door behind her. 'See that man. Do you see that man? He's a . . . '

'Don't swear,' said Clarissa.

'I never swear. When have I ever sworn?'

'Well, don't start now,' said Clarissa, 'and calm down. We need to get on with this. You wouldn't let me blow my lid like that.'

Macleod went to react, but as per usual, she'd backed him into a corner. One in which he'd have to admit she was completely correct. Macleod just felt his fuse was being shortened every time he spoke to the new DCI. Generally, in his career, he'd got on well with superior officers, but this one—this one just drove him nuts.

He let out a sigh. 'Sit down,' he said. 'What have you got?'

'Just had Ross on the phone. Apparently, Dr Jacobs had a fancy woman coming in. They'd spend time in his office. He'd nip out every once in a while, go and get champagne and lunch and that; she had free access to all the files.'

'So, what does she look like?'

'Well, we got a sketch up, but the secretary said she never saw her face fully. The woman always arrived with a hood or a scarf on, glasses. It was all apparently because of her husband, but the secretary swears the woman didn't have a husband. Said there was a false ring on her finger. She'd seen underneath it and there wasn't any ring mark.'

'Would explain how she could get into his room,' said Macleod. 'The woman down in Glasgow, she was scarfed up with glasses. Do we know if they're the same glasses?'

'Unsure, but they seem to be similar. We got the sketch through from what the secretary had seen. We also got the sketch done from Dr Green. Trying to compile them together because they certainly look very alike. The boys are trying to make it into an image we can take round.

'Well, when we do, we'd probably want to get that down to Dr Stephens. See if she's seen anyone similar.'

'It's going to be hard though,' said Clarissa, 'to trace a face and a dress. Even if she does know her, will she know her well enough? How will she know her? Where will she know her from? There must be some other way of connecting in.'

Macleod sat back in his chair. 'A lot of these victims, they won a prize to go on the ferry. It looks like they were set up to be on the ferry. Now, we had our ferry worker who died as well. It's my guess that they were setting everything to look like some sort of ferry suicide or someone who'd have an issue with a ferry or some sort of angst because the ferries have just been cancelled. Maybe they were looking to push us in that direction.'

'When they got the prizes though, they had won them,' said Clarissa. 'If you got a letter through the post, you'd expect it to have some sort of address on it. If they contacted them by phone, they'd still need details. We're not quite sure how they all won. Are we?'

'But those that received it are dead,' said Macleod. 'Get on the phone, Clarissa. Phone back the partners of all the victims, those who received ferry tickets, see how they arrived. See if they spoke on the phone because we know some did, but the number it went to was an old number, but if you got a prize, it would have something on it, an initial response. See if any of them didn't contact by phone, maybe contacted in a different way—email, something else because they had to give details, didn't they? Give details so they could get the tickets. Get booked with the passenger details, cars.'

'Will do, Seoras,' said Clarissa, standing up. 'Are you okay to calm down now?'

'I'm just going to ring Hope,' he said. 'Put her in line with what's happened overnight. I think she needs to try and get her eye on Dr Stephens. She's the one doctor we've got remaining. She could very much be at risk.'

Clarissa went back to the main office, sat down, and picked up the phone. The first person she called was Marie Culshaw and asked about any correspondence that had been left behind. Andrew had picked them all up though. Andrew had done everything with the ferry; that's the way he was. She spent ten minutes rooting around the house, but there was nothing, no detail, so Clarissa thanked her and moved on to her next call. She placed a call in to Fred Martin's brother, and also to Constable Alan McNair but neither of them had any paperwork around how Fred had won his prize to go on the trip, so Clarissa decided to ring Gerald Lyndhurst.

'Hello, Detective. I did speak to you when you were down. It's been quite hard getting anything of Peter's, but I can see if I can get to his house. Have a look.'

'Was he orderly enough? Would he have kept them anyway?' asked Clarissa.

'I don't know, probably. He did like that. He did make sure he hung onto things.'

'Give me an hour.'

Clarissa twiddled her thumbs while Gerald Lyndhurst was presumably entering the house of Peter Hughes. He had a key but maybe the man was still unsure about going in. An hour later, Clarissa received a call back.

'Detective Sergeant, this is Gerald. I've been round to Peter's. Went through a lot of personal documentation and to be honest, it was quite difficult. I didn't actually find any of the tickets. I did find the initial letter, that he'd won the prize.'

'Have you got it with you?' asked Clarissa.

'Yes, I do. I don't see anything in particular. It has a phone number for him to call. I think that's how he did it.'

'Has it got anything more than a phone number? Anything you would say, like an address?'

The man scanned. 'It does say that you can send it to an address here . . . , well, it's not an address; it's a post office box.

'Can you let me know what it is?' Clarissa made a note of

the post office box. It says, 'It's Glasgow, the post office box,' said the man. 'I don't know if he wrote to that or not.'

'Regardless, that's very handy. Do you know how to scan documents?' asked Clarissa.

'Of course. Shall I send it up to you?'

'Please do,' she said and passed on the email address for Gerald Lyndhurst to send up a captured copy of the initial document. Five minutes later, Clarissa sat with it in front of her. It had clearly been done to look quite professional. It did, indeed, give the option of contacting via the post office box. The telephone number on it they had checked before, and it was a pay-as-you-go, untraceable, but the post office box wouldn't have been so easy. Hope picked up her telephone and called the Glasgow headquarters of the post office. It took her a moment to get through to the right person, but once she had, she inquired about who the post office box belonged to.

'Detective Sergeant, this is Greg here with the post office. Yes, I've looked up that post office box number for you and I've got an address, it's down in Glasgow.'

'When was it opened up?'

'Been there for about four years. I'm not sure how much correspondence comes through it, or who picks it up. I can get you through to some of the local workers. They might be able to tell you.'

'That's brilliant,' said Clarissa and she took down the address in the Bellshill area of Glasgow. 'I'll just patch you through,' said Greg. 'Just give me a minute.'

Clarissa hung on the call and could see Macleod looking out from his office towards her. She gave a wave with her hand and the Inspector made his way over to her desk. He was about to speak when Clarissa put her hand up, a single finger to her

185

mouth indicating he should be quiet. She was aware that the other constables in the room who were helping them with the inquiry seemed to look sheepishly away, believing that this was not something you did to Macleod.

'Hello, this is Emily. Are you the detective?'

'Yes, I am,' said Clarissa, and gave the post office box number that she was inquiring about.

'Just give me a moment and I'll ask amongst the staff.' While Clarissa hung on the phone, she advised Macleod of what she was doing, and she could see the excitement rising within him.

'This is Emily again. I've spoken to a couple of our colleagues, and apparently, it's a woman that comes in for that. We know because she always wears big sunglasses, even in the height of winter and a big hood or a scarf on.

'What colour hair does she have?' asked Clarissa.

'Well, that's the thing. We were just saying that. The hair keeps changing. It can be blonde, it can be a brunette, sometimes it's red. Quite bizarre, really, isn't it?'

'Does she have a name?'

'Kerry Watson. I believe you've got the address that the post office box is linked to.'

'We do,' said Clarissa. 'If I send someone round, do you think your colleagues could describe them to them so we can make up a sort of a photofit picture?'

'Of course,' said Emily. 'Just ask for Emily at this office. I'll be aware of what's going on.'

Clarissa came off the phone and could see Macleod hovering over her desk.

'That address is a post office box on the bottom of the initial competition letter. Gerald Lyndhurst retrieved it from Peter Hughes's house. I've checked the Post Office box and it belongs to Kerry Watson. I think that's a false name, but there's an address attached to it.'

'I think it's time we get Hope round there. Where is it again?' Macleod looked at the address. 'Not the most salubrious area,' he said, remembering from his many years spent down in Glasgow. 'In fact, I think nowadays it's quite a run-down sort of place with lots of boarded-up houses.'

'Ideal then,' said Clarissa. 'If you wanted a false address or somewhere you didn't have people go very often. If you are you going to send Hope round, what do we do?' asked Clarissa.

'You're going to go and get that little sports car of yours,' said Macleod. 'We're going on a trip down to Glasgow.'

'You think it's wise to all go down there? She was just here recently.'

'Yes. There was a woman in here last night. She got scared off. She's not going to come back towards Dr Green at the moment. Too much heat around him. She'll head back to what else she needs to sort out. If she's realised we're onto Dr Green, and Dr Jacobs has just been killed, then we need to have a look at Dr Stephens. I think she's heading that way. We also might be able to catch her heading to that address for she could be down in Glasgow already. Besides, Ross can get back here. Won't take him long to get across from Aberdeen. He can hold the fort while you and I make our way down.'

'There's got to be some stronger connection though, hasn't there? What's tying it in? Why these three? Why going through people who are trying to help couples? Why were they focusing on the member of that couple who seemed to break everything up? There's a history going on here.'

'It's more than that. They've got to be able to use ketamine and use it properly. Maybe we need to start looking at it from the angle of the doctors and people who belong to them. Dr Jacobs didn't previously know the person that was coming to him so she couldn't have worked for him. Dr Green has offered nothing up, but I doubt he knew her before or he would would have said at the start of the liasions. Dr Stephens is the one that we don't know if she's been intimate with her. Therefore, she might be the one doctor that this person is connected to in a different way.'

'And this person will know that we'll have a description of her from Dr Green.'

'Exactly,' said Macleod, 'I'm banking on her going down for Stephens. Especially if the heat's on and we find her base.'

'Well, I'll get the car then,' said Clarissa. 'Make sure you bring your coat. Don't want you complaining about the hood being down again.'

Macleod shook his head and strode away. He was like a bloodhound. As soon as the scent hit his nose, he was off, the weariness of the night thrown away. Clarissa, on the other hand, was thinking about stocking up with coffee for the long drive south.

Chapter 23

After finishing her call with Macleod, Hope placed another call to Dr Stevens's surgery in an attempt to locate the woman. Her secretary announced that she was there and put her through.

'Detective Sergeant, what can I do for you?' asked Dr Stevens.

'I think you may be in danger,' said Hope. 'I don't know if you've realised or seen the news, but there was a murder last night in a hotel. Dr Jacobs, who we went to see, was killed in his hotel room by a female we're currently looking for. I've got some pictures and images I want you to have a look at.'

'Okay. I am pretty busy though. I think I'm booked up with consultations all day.'

'If you can make the time to have a look and give me a call if you think it's anyone significant.'

'So, what? You have a person you want me to look at?'

'A picture. We're trying to establish a picture of the person who killed Dr Jacobs. I want to know if you've seen this person before.'

'Okay. I'll try and take a look, but I'm just about to go in with a couple, for a couple of hours, then there'll be lunch. By the time I'm getting back from that, we'll see. Send it through to my secretary and I'll take a look though.'

Hope came off the phone call, believing that the woman wasn't taking her seriously enough. She'd have to go round after she'd visited the address acquired from the post office with regards to the PO box in Glasgow. Hope exited the Glasgow station and dropped by at the hotel just to see if there had been any more developments before departing for the Bellshill address.

The address took Hope into a street that looked almost deserted. Out of the twenty houses, she counted sixteen which were boarded up. One didn't have any boards and possibly it was a squat, for she could see some people inside with sleeping bags. The other three houses, of which one was a flat on top of another house, seemed to be occupied to some degree. She found out the flat was the address she was looking for and climbed the outside stairs up to the front door, banging it loudly. When no one answered, she pushed the door with a little force, finding that the lock slid off and the door opened.

Well, that's unusual, thought Hope. *I guess I better check there's no one inside in trouble.*

She stepped onto the carpet announcing that she was the police and was there anyone home, but there came no answer. She looked at a sofa with mould on it. It was damp, white spots running across the top of it. The whole room stank. Reaching down to the floor, Hope found a carpet that was also damp. She could see the walls had mould and the light fitting was gone.

Had people broken in? What was with that? Hope walked through the small hall to the front of the house to see a kitchen, again, smelling like nobody had been in it in a long time. There was a cracked plate in the sink. She tried the tap and found out the water didn't work. A flick of a switch filled the room with light, but the light bulb was hanging on its own with no cover.

She just used this as a drop, thought Hope, *just a random address, but if they sent it to her, she'd have to pick it up. She must have checked, whoever she is.*

Hope was glad she was wearing her boots, because she wasn't sure about the floor as she found a small bedroom at the rear. She almost vomited at the state of the bed. *Rat poo on that*, she thought, *and maybe even human excrement, and look at the state of the sheet, ripped and eaten.*

Hope saw a door with a padlock on it, at the far side of the room. She stepped back out into the main living room and tried to work out the angles to see how big the room the door led to would be. *Big enough for a small office*, thought Hope, *big enough to sit in quite easily, accommodate maybe computers, a couple of chairs, big enough to house something.*

Hope reached inside her jacket and dug out a few skeleton keys. The lock didn't seem to be particularly advanced, and she easily opened the lock, taking it off, and then opening the door. Inside was dark and Hope took out her pen torch, skimming around the inside of the room. She was right. The room was approximately three feet square and had a computer, a printer, and a number of boards on the walls with lots of pictures.

Hope flashed the light up and saw the face of Fred Martin. One of his wife as well. She could see Dr Jacobs with his wife. Marie Culshaw's face appeared, tagged in to Andrew's, and above it was Daphne Walsh. Hope scanned again and saw Gerald Lyndhurst, Paul Hughes beside him, and up above was Jenny Trimble. Many of the figures had an X on them, including that of Dr Jacobs.

Hope reached into her jacket, took out some gloves, keen not to contaminate the scene. She looked up above her with her light and saw a single bulb hanging, and then flicked her own light around the small room, trying to find a switch. A thought occurred to her. Hope stepped outside into the bedroom and flicked on the switch at the side of the room. The bedroom light didn't come on but the light inside the small room with the pictures did.

Clever girl, thought Hope. *Bypassed, made this look like a real dump. She's worked hard at this. Clearly, whoever it was, lived somewhere else, but this is where she planned things from. This is where she operated from and what a place. A house nobody would look through twice stuck on a street that was practically abandoned.* Hope placed a call to Macleod.

'Good work,' said Macleod. 'Get a forensic team down. Check it through. Can you see anything of note, anywhere else we know she could be going? Anything that refers to her home address or even who she is?'

'Not so far, Seoras. I haven't looked through everything, but there's photocopied images here of doctors' notes. Whole histories of the people that have died. There was also a red ring around faces. Usually, those to be killed. You can see from here how she set the whole thing up.'

'Is there anything that tells us who she is?' asked Macleod.

'Nothing,' said Hope, 'nothing. I'm willing to bet even when she used here, she put gloves on, wrapped her hair up, made sure she didn't leave too much of a trace. Even if you picked any DNA up, you wonder if she's even on any database. It's a sloppy piece of work, the post office box. I guess she thought we would come and look at this and think, 'No'. There was excrement on the bed. Everything to make you walk back out of this house. Part of me thinks it was planted,' said Hope.

'Well, we're on our way,' said Macleod. 'I'm with Clarissa, so we won't be long,'

Hope gave a little chuckle. 'Good, Seoras. Because I'm worried. I'm worried if she's actually succeeded in doing everything she wanted to do, or is there more?'

'What do you mean?' asked Macleod.

'Well, she rang Dr Jacobs here and I'm wondering are there any other figures? I'll keep searching and get back to you.'

Hope hung up the call and continued to look through the items. There was much paperwork, lots of photographs, and Hope worked tirelessly to go through them. At the bottom of the pile, she found a photograph of what looked like a younger Dr Stevens, maybe from ten years ago. She swallowed hard as she saw a ring around the doctor's face. Hope took a photograph of it, and she heard the forensic team arriving outside.

Stepping out of the flat in order to take a breath of fresh air, Hope called the local Glasgow station, asking that they put a plainclothes officer outside Dr Stevens's office and keep an eye on her, especially for any women fitting the picture that she was sending to them. The picture was that of the composite that had been produced up in Inverness from the various images of the woman with sunglasses.

Hope then showed the forensic team around and slowly, they began to bag everything up. It was well after lunch by the time Hope had finished searching through all the items, aware now that Dr Stevens was a possible target. She'd also seen Dr Green in an image with his face ringed. Clearly, Clarissa had done the right thing. Hope called Macleod back.

'She's definitely lined up the doctor, Seoras. I realise that now, I put a plainclothes policeman outside her office to look especially for any women that came in matching a height of five feet seven. I'm going to go round and find the doctor myself, have a word, and see if she knows of anyone who would have anything against her. More specifically, to find out if she's got a female lover. After all, that's the way this killer moved in on the other doctors.'

'Good idea,' said Macleod. 'Clarissa is breaking who knows how many speed limits; we'll be with you very shortly, but we'll route to the office as well. I want to speak to her too. If she realises she's being guarded, our killer might just cut and run.'

'Okay, Seoras. I'll play it cool. I'll just pop round. Just see if we still got the plainclothes person there.'

Hope thanked the forensic team and left them working. Getting back into her car, she drove round to Dr Stevens's practice. It was now close to three o'clock, and as Hope strode up the steps to enter the practice, she could see a man standing in the far corner. She walked over to him directly, making him rather agitated until she said, 'Detective Sergeant Hope McGrath, I placed you here. Anything to report?'

'No. The doctor was in earlier on, I'm still right here. She hasn't come out at all.'

'Okay,' said Hope, 'I'm going to go in and talk to her. Stick around in case I need you.'

The man nodded and Hope made her way into the practice approaching Dr Stevens's secretary who recognised her.

'You're too late,' she said, 'she's gone. She was a bit bothered though. I did tell her she should call you.'

'Call me? Why?'

'There's a man outside. He's been there most of the day. She was agitated about him, so she opened up one of the rear windows and went out that way.'

'How long ago did she disappear?'

'Twenty minutes. She was heading for an early dinner in a café close to here. She was going to walk round.'

'Do you have that address?' asked Hope.

'Why? Is she in trouble?'

For a moment, Hope thought about giving out too much information, but then she thought, *what the heck?* 'Yes, she's in trouble. I need to ascertain her whereabouts and get close to her as soon as possible.'

'I'll just dig up the reservation for you. Hang on.' The woman disappeared into her computer before scribbling down an address and handing it over to Hope. 'That's it. That's where she was meeting. It's like a café that serves quite decent, quality food. It's a bit posh.'

'Do you know if she was meeting anyone?'

'Yes. She said she was, but she didn't tell me who it was, just that she'd be heading off at this time for dinner.'

Hope thanked the woman for the address, turned and marched out of the centre and found the plainclothes officer approaching her shoulder. 'Do you want me to stay in case she leaves?' he asked.

'No point. She left over twenty minutes ago. Just go back to the station.'

Hope saw a look of bemusement on the man's face, but she issued the instruction again, and he walked away. Hope jumped into her car, looked up her mapping system, and input the address of the café. It was a couple of minutes' drive and she placed a call to Macleod. She could hear the rush of the wind and Clarissa must have been driving with the top down, and she could also hear noise of traffic.

'She's gone, Seoras. Dr Stevens has gone out. She's gone to have her meal and is meeting somebody, but we don't know who. I'm on my way there. It'll only take me a couple of minutes. You need to route to this address.' Hope rhymed off where she was going. Hope could hear a simple 'understood' from Macleod, who then shouted at Clarissa to drive hard. For once, there was no comeback from the woman and the call closed down. Hope turned her engine on, spun the wheel, and drove right into the traffic, racing along a number of streets to her destination.

Her mind raced. *Will Dr Stevens still be there? The killer has got to her first. Why hasn't she stayed in her office? I had her protected. I had her safe. Does the woman not realise the issues that were going on here? People have died.* But there was nothing she could do about that now. Hope simply kept the accelerator pressed and swerved in and out of traffic as she raced to her destination.

Chapter 24

Hope raced through Glasgow before parking up the car a short distance from the café she'd been advised of by Dr Stephens's secretary. Her eyes scanned the street, looking for anyone untoward outside of the café but she could see no one, so continued to walk at pace to a small set of steps that led up into the dining area. As she entered, a woman dressed smartly in black trousers and a waistcoat stopped her, asking if she required a table. Hope didn't look at her. Instead, she surveyed the room, while taking her credentials out from inside her leather jacket and holding them up in front of the woman.

'I'm here to see Dr Stephens. She's booked a table with someone. I'm not sure if it's in her name or the other person's name. The other person I don't know.'

'Well, there's no Dr Stephens dining here. Can you see her in the room?'

'Yes, I can. I'll just go directly to her if that's okay with you? She's at a table over there.'

'Is there anything else I can assist you with?' asked the woman.

'Actually, who booked the table? The one that Dr Stephens

is sitting at.'

'That would be in the name of Steele. I'm not quite sure if it's a man or a woman, but in the name of Steele.'

'Thank you,' said Hope and walked across the dining area between tables, keeping an eye out for anyone sitting at them. It was only after three in the afternoon, so it was a quiet time, and there were only four other people in the restaurant. There was a young couple who seemed deeply engrossed in each other, while an older couple were sitting looking at their mobile phones. Hope put her hand up, waving over at Dr Stephens who raised her head up from a mineral water she was drinking and smiled.

'Why did you leave?' asked Hope. 'You were safe at work; we were keeping an eye on you there. I put a man out the front.'

'Yes, there was a guy standing there the whole time. Kept watching, looking over everything. I thought it might have been the person coming after me, so I left.'

'But you should have called,' said Hope, 'if you thought that, you could have checked with me. You could have said, 'I've got somebody dodgy out here,' and we would have sent someone round, or in that case, I'd have said to you, 'That's our man.''

'Oh, I'm sorry. I didn't want to bother you, in case it was a wild goose chase, which obviously it turns out it was. I just slipped out the back, came out to here. It's only my secretary who knows I'm coming here.'

'And the person you're coming to meet,' said Hope, 'they're aware as well.'

'Yes, actually it was a call out of the blue, a bit of a surprise. Alice Steele used to work for me. God love her, she was a poor critter. Felt a lot for her. Anyway, she sounded quite upset so I thought I'd best go and speak to her.'

'When was the last time you saw her?'

'Oh, four years ago,' said Dr Stephens, 'or is it five? She used to work for me as my secretary before we got Janine, the new one. Alice, she was a good secretary, but she had a lot of problems in life. God love her, she struggled. I was kind of hoping when I see her that she might have gone on a bit, moved on.'

'Is that all she was, though? Just your secretary?'

'Well, I did help her a bit with her husband. She was a poor critter. I don't even know why she wanted him; there were rumours that he ran off, I heard a couple of years ago. It doesn't surprise me. They never seemed to get on properly. I shouldn't say anymore, you know, patient confidentiality and all that. She still is alive after all. It's not like I'm telling you something about somebody who's dead.'

'What time are you to meet her?' asked Hope.

'Any time now.'

'Good,' said Hope, 'I've been up all night. I'm actually quite hungry. I'll sit here with you if you don't mind.'

'Aren't you meant to be sort of plainclothes looking after me? Not get in the way of people's life?'

'We tried that, didn't we?' said Hope. 'You walked out the back door, or the back window to be precise. If you're going to be that slippery a customer, I'm going to eat with you.' Hope raised her hand and waved at the maître d, who disappeared off to get a second mineral water.

'Tell me more about Alice Steele,' said Hope. 'What did she do before she became your secretary? Was she in the medical profession? I heard a lot of secretaries in your work start off in medical professions before they change roles.'

'That is true. We do sometimes get ex-nurses. People who

trained up and didn't feel it was for them but still wanted or needed to get a job. Quite often the medical background can help if you're operating as a secretary.'

'Was that the case with Alice?'

'She wasn't a medical nurse. I believe she was actually in the military. That's right. She never actually qualified, was a trainee military nurse. I could never work out whether it was her husband, or if it was actually the military that she couldn't hack. You'd have thought if it was her husband she would have stayed in, but maybe it was because he was quite abusive with her, told her what she should do. Like I say, I heard he disappeared, possibly ran off with another woman.'

'Did she say why she wanted to meet you now?'

'No, not at all.'

'As your secretary,' asked Hope, 'would Alice have had any access to your records?'

'Almost all. She'd have filed doctor's notes, everything. Much the same as Janine does now. You have to trust these people; it's part and parcel of it. They work with you, they don't make comment, they don't pass out anything about anyone else.'

'Would they be able to access what's in your office now?'

'Well, Janine would of course. She has the keys to access all the locked-up material; that's because I need her to. I need her sometimes to go and get files for me. Sometimes if I'm away, she runs the office. She needs to pull out confidential information.'

'You mean like addresses, histories, things like that?'

'Totally.'

'Did Alice have access to that?' asked Hope.

'Completely. Just the same as Janine.'

'And did she have a set of keys?'

'There are two set of keys, Janine has one, and I have the original set. Prior to Janine having hers, Alice had them before she handed them to Janine.'

'You didn't feel that you needed to change the locks or anything?'

'Why? These are medical professionals. I trusted Alice for all those years. She then handed her keys in. Why would I be worried about her?'

Hope could see the picture emerging.

'This address,' said Hope, pushing a piece of paper in front of her with the address of the flat that she'd come from earlier on it, 'do you recognise it?'

'Bellshill,' said Dr Stephens, 'that's where Alice used to live. Yes. That's the old house, I think. It was a flat, wasn't it? A type of flat. Got a bit rougher now.'

'I've just come from that flat. I've just tied that flat to the recent murders we've been having.'

Dr Stephens looked up, shock spreading across her face. 'You think somebody's got to Alice? You don't think that they've got information from her?'

'No,' said Hope. 'I don't think anybody's got to Alice. I think Alice has got to a lot of other people but by the sounds of it, she was coming here to meet you. Dr Jacobs is dead. She went for Dr Green as well in Inverness, but my colleague turned up; otherwise, he'd be dead. I think she's coming for you now. Get your coat, Dr Stephens; we're not staying.'

Stephens looked agitated, but she turned around, grabbed her handbag, and pulled her jacket on before putting her handbag over her shoulder. Hope looked round and saw the maître d' bringing a woman towards her. *Approximate height,* thought Hope, *five feet seven. The hair. There's no hair, no long hair.* In fact, the woman was wearing a small beanie hat.

'That,' said Dr Stephens, 'is Alice,' over Hope's shoulder.

'Are you sure? What colour hair does she have?'

'She's got alopecia. She lost her hair quite a while ago, one of the problems with her husband, I believe—so unfair on her.'

Hope stepped across the room to meet Alice head-on, but the woman had her hand in her pocket of a jacket and lifted the jacket up pointing it towards Hope.

'That wasn't you in Inverness, was it?' said the woman, her voice was gravelly, almost husky.

'But it was you, wasn't it?' said Hope. 'Sunglasses, wigs, one minute you're blonde, then you're brunette, then red, whatever you want to be.'

'Well, I didn't get any of my own, or I did and then it disappeared. Go sit down, whoever you are. I need to talk to Dr Stephens.'

Hope edged backwards slowly into her seat as the woman came and stood a few feet away, her jacket lifted out in front of her, and Hope could see where a gun was pointed from inside the pocket at Dr Stephens.

'Alice, what is this? I thought you'd got on with things. I thought you'd changed.'

'Changed? Me? I didn't get the chance to change, did I? I came to you when I was in trouble. Could you help me? No.'

'I tried, but if the other side isn't willing . . . , and then I heard he ran off.'

'He didn't run anywhere, I just got wise to it. I just got to the point where I decided that I was having no more of it. He's gone now; he's not coming back.'

'But what are you doing? Why are you doing this? Why me?'

'Well, I was going to close off the loop. I had to move quick. You see, they started to find things out. I went wrong somewhere and suddenly there was heat everywhere. I took out Jacobs and almost Green. It was easy to get out of them all about the people they looked after. I remembered you talking about them. Oh yeah, that day at the conference, how great you guys were. How you'll solve all these issues. You solved nothing.

'You didn't solve anything for Marie Culshaw. You didn't solve anything for Una Martin—she died, committed suicide. You didn't solve anything for the Walsh man either; he suffered. That Jenny Trimble, she was playing around, same as my man, nobody stopped that. Nobody got them to turn around. I realised they're just bad eggs. Meanwhile, you people, you're just making money off us. Making money off the ones that suffer but I was able to get the real picture from their information, able to find out who was at fault, go and sort it for them, before you took away any more money.'

'And now you're closing off the loop,' said Hope. 'There's no point. You'd be better running now. Better just get out of here.'

'You can shut up. I didn't ask for your opinion. I could shoot you first. Maybe I'll have to. Stand up.'

Hope got to her feet slowly. 'Now turn around.' With her hands in the air, Hope turned. There was a hard blow across the back of her head, and she tumbled forward, hitting a chair before spinning; then everything was dark.

* * *

Clarissa Urquhart pulled the car in to a small space just down from their destination. Hope had told them where the café was and Macleod was out of the car before Clarissa had even finished switching off the engine. Macleod ran along the street, Clarissa fighting to keep up with him. Then she watched him stop dead, an arm put out.

'Easy,' he said, 'look. Look in the window.'

Clarissa looked past Macleod and could see Dr Stephens with someone behind her.

'There's a gun in that pocket,' said Macleod. 'Look at the way it's shaped. Where's Hope, where the heck's McGrath gone?'

'Stay cool, Seoras. If that's a gun, we don't want to be getting in front of it.'

'If that's a gun, and she takes her away from here, the woman's dead,' said Macleod. 'Who knows what she's done with Hope? I'm going to go in the front door.'

'Don't be an idiot. What's that going to achieve?'

'I'll talk her down. I'll talk her down and I want you to go around the back just in case she cuts loose.'

'Like the blazes, I'm coming up there with you.'

'I gave you an order, Sergeant. You do what I've just said.'

'Don't put yourself in line of fire like this. We'll call for backup.'

'She's coming out the door, there's no time. Stephens will be dead if she gets out of here.'

Clarissa looked at Macleod, and could see that he made his mind up on what he was going to do. She turned and tried to half sprint around the end of the street corner into an alley at the back. She was no runner, and she thought she could lurk at the back door in case the woman came out that way. As she made her way along the backstreet and into the rear of the kitchen, Clarissa wondered if that would be enough. Macleod was placing himself out front, putting himself into danger.

She entered a kitchen that had a lot of staff at the door, the main thoroughfare leading through to the dining room. Clarissa approached them.

'Kindly step back. I know your eyes are fixed on what's going on in there, but I'm Detective Sergeant Clarissa Urquhart, and I need to get through.'

A chef turned at her, looked at her bizarrely before turning back. She put a hand on his shoulder, 'Move,' she said, 'do it quietly. Slowly.' The kitchen staff retreated from the door as Clarissa reached it, pushing it forward, carefully stepping inside the dining room. Clarissa could see that the gun was now out of the woman's pocket and being held up to the rear of the head of Dr Stephens. Macleod was speaking, but he was doing it quietly, and Clarissa could barely hear. She cast a glance to her right and saw Hope McGrath on the ground, a pool of blood coming from the back of her head.

Clarissa wondered what to do. She crouched down as best as she could, slowly creeping her way forward through the dining room. Macleod had crept his way in, closing the door of the restaurant behind him and was standing in front of the large glass windows which he and Clarissa had looked in through just a few minutes before. She watched as the woman pressed the back of Dr Stephens, forcing her to step forward toward Macleod. The conversation seemed to be getting more heated, even if it was quiet and then Clarissa saw Macleod step in front of Stephens.

'No, you won't,' he said loudly. 'Don't do it.'

'I've killed enough already; what's another one or two going to matter?'

The woman's left hand moved towards the weapon and

Clarissa didn't stop to think, she sprang forward, running as hard as she could, shouting at the woman. The gun turned around, facing Clarissa now, but she put her shoulder down in something reminiscent of a rugby tackle. Without thought, she threw her left shoulder into the woman's abdomen, taking her off her feet and together they hit the window with enough force that it shattered.

Clarissa fell, tumbling over, her back hitting something on the ground, arms flailing out. Her wrist hit something solid as she cried out in pain. Clarissa found herself looking up at the sky, and she turned her head to see where the gunwoman had fallen. An arm shot across, grabbing Clarissa by the throat, and she began to choke, but there was a cry from above her and a foot stomped down hard on the woman's arm, causing her to release the chokehold she had.

Clarissa looked into the face of Macleod, but he was all concentration, pulling the woman's arms behind her, slapping cuffs on her and making sure that the gun was well out of the way. He kept one knee on the woman's back, looking down at Clarissa.

'Are you okay? Are you all right?'

Clarissa tried to get up, but the whole of her body ached. 'No,' said Clarissa, 'I'm not okay. The last time I went through a window, I was twenty-three.'

Macleod looked down at her. 'Twenty-three? What were you doing, woman?' he asked.

'Alcohol, Seoras. Bad days, trust me. Bad days.'

Chapter 25

'Are you sure she's all right?'

'Stop fussing, Seoras. I'm fine. It's just a little out of sync.'

'It's not a little out of sync. They said you tore something in your shoulder. It's torn. It's not out of sync. It needs assistance; it needs to be looked at. You need to be looked after.'

'If you don't shut up, I'll kick you through a window,' said Clarissa and gave Macleod a hard stare.

'I'm responsible for your welfare. You were injured on duty. We'll get you in the car and take you back up to Inverness, but you're on several weeks' rest and recuperation. What were you thinking going through that window anyway?'

'Well, thanks. She pointed a gun at you. She was going to kill you. What do you mean what was I thinking?'

'You took her out the window. You could've just grabbed her arm, put the gun up into the air. I could've run to assist.'

'Hope,' said Clarissa, 'take him away. Get him out of this room or I'm going to throttle him.'

Hope McGrath stepped into the fray with a wry smile on her face. 'Sir,' she said, trying to appease Macleod, 'I believe Ross wants you on the phone outside.'

'He's on the line?' asked Macleod.

'No. He was calling, though. I think he wants you to speak to him.'

'What about?'

'Something to do with the investigation,' said Hope. Macleod looked quizzical but made his way out of the small room in the Glasgow Medical Centre.

'Ross doesn't want anything, does he?' said Clarissa.

'Nope, but I hope he plays it. Why didn't you just tell him?'

'Tell him what?'

'Macleod, tell him why you took her through the window. You acted on impulse. It was him. You went to save him.'

'Yes,' said Clarissa, 'I did, and look at me. Look at me, the daft bird. Torn this, torn that. I'm not going to be able to drive. You realise that, don't you?'

'Yes. The streets of Inverness will be safer for a while at least.'

'How are you doing, anyway?' asked Clarissa.

'Bump on the head. A pretty big bump on the head, but a bump in the head. It was a bit of a bleeder. They put some stitches in, but I'm fine. A week's time and I'll not even know it's there.'

'Good,' said Clarissa. 'The woman was scary, wasn't she?'

'I wouldn't have said she was scary,' said Hope. 'She was someone who just had everything stacked up against her. It seems that after being kicked out from her role as a military nurse, she became a secretary but then her father divorced from her mother. He was abusive to her mother, and Alice saw most of it. It was a bad divorce that had left her mom penniless. Alice managed to come out of that, became a secretary, and then got married. She was then cheated on. They say he ran off, or at least, that's what Dr Stevens said.'

'What do you mean that's what she says? Doesn't anybody know?'

'Yes, Sergeant Urquhart,' interrupted Macleod, 'Alice said she killed him.'

Hope looked around the white walls of the room as if anything would be preferable to Macleod's face. He'd been listening.

'I think you got the wrong end of the stick, Hope. Ross didn't seem to know what you were talking about. Banging your head must have been worse than we thought.'

'Indeed,' said Hope, 'Clarissa was just asking about Alice's husband. At least, Dr Stevens said that Alice's husband, Alan, seemed to be of a slightly different vein.'

'Once we took her in, Sergeant, she told us. He's underneath the floorboards of the Bellshill flat. There were so many other things in there that stank, it didn't really make much difference. It's been a day or two of quite disturbing interviews,' said Macleod. 'I feel for the woman. She had it rough. Her husband was running around on her, her father had left them, her mother had ended up destitute, and she just snapped because those people that were meant to put the world right, the Dr Stevenses, Dr Jacobses, and the Dr Greens of this world, they didn't. Charged a fortune for it. She saw it all too often.'

'But they do sort some things out, don't they?' said Clarissa.

'Of course, they do,' said Macleod, 'but not from where she was standing. Not her situation. She lost it, but she decided other people should lose it for that. She wasn't daft. She was going to set up a cover. It would be suicides. People killing themselves off the ferries. Her ploy was good, except we recovered some bodies and we got them quickly. If we hadn't been able to realise it was Ketamine in the system, find the needle marks, we wouldn't have suspected anything. We'd have gone along with a strange state of suicides.

'Just people seeing a way out after other people have done it. After all, all those that died had plenty of black marks on their copybook, didn't they? Cheating, forcing other people to do things. That's why she went after them. You can easily see the guilty, but we got her, at the end of the day. We managed to find out. The hardest part of it was, after all of this, getting a "Well done" from the DCI. Said it was brilliant the way I've spoken to him the whole way through, kept him in the loop.'

Hope stared at Macleod, 'You didn't?'

'I did.'

Clarissa looked across, 'Did what?'

'I told him what I thought of him. I told him how badly he played this.'

'How did he take that?' asked Hope.

'Well,' said Macleod, 'have you been wanting to become a Detective Inspector because there might be an opening coming up?'

'How come?'

'Well, he basically said he was there to stay. I would have to like or lump it. Either that or get out of the station.'

'You'll see him gone,' said Hope, 'of course, you will.' She tapped Macleod on the shoulder, but she could see he was thinking.

As Hope left the room, Clarissa kept studying Macleod's face. 'Don't go because of somebody else,' she said; 'never go because of somebody else. You don't let them chase you out. You walk out on your own terms when you're ready.'

'Well, thank you for that advice,' said Macleod, 'but next time, if I need it, I will ask.

'You don't have to ask,' said Clarissa; 'it's always free as well from me.' She was sitting on a chair, and she watched as Macleod came over closer to her.

'Look,' he said, 'I just wanted to say.' Clarissa looked up and saw the man's face moving towards her. He reached up with his hand, touched the side of her head, and placed a kiss on her forehead. 'That was reckless, way too reckless, but thank you.'

'You mean a lot to me, Seoras. You mean a lot to the team.'

'And a lot to me,' he said, 'but next time, just let me deal with it. I don't put you at risk like that.'

'Then next time, don't put me out there.' She watched him smile at her.

'I did wonder when you came on board, was I doing the right thing? I think, so far, it's been a good idea.'

When he turned away, she reached to give him a slap on the back. It connected with next to no force and she grimaced.

'Just get me out of this darn room,' she said, 'I've been sat here, pushed, and prodded to be told that I don't feel great. I knew that. I knew I needed rest, so let's get going.'

'I thought I would run your car up to Inverness. You could travel with Hope, in hers.'

'You're not driving my car up. There's no way. You take Hope's car and I'll drive up with Hope.'

'You can't drive,' said Macleod. 'Doctor said, "No driving." Hope's not familiar with your car anyway. I'm more used to it. After all, you've raced me up around here, there, and everywhere recently. Better if I drive it. I've seen how you handle it. Probably best if we show you how to take care of a car.'

Macleod was out through the door before Clarissa could

reach him. She winced in pain, and she stretched for him but she shouldn't have. Racing through the room, she saw Hope look at her.

'He's taking my car. He's going to drive me to bloody Inverness.'

'What's wrong with that?' asked Hope.

'We'll be hours. Have you seen him drive?'

'He said you needed to learn the speed limit,' said Hope and laughed as she saw Clarissa in agony, running out of the hospital after Macleod, but as she saw them both go, Hope felt a shiver. They'd been lucky. She'd been lucky. All she wanted to do now was jump in the car and head home. John would be waiting, and she thanked whoever was out there, whoever helped look after her in this life, that at least her relationship was good. She'd seen enough bad ones to last her a lifetime.

Read on to discover the Patrick Smythe series!

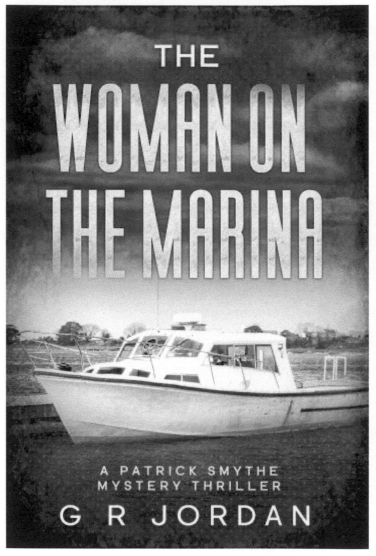

Start your Patrick Smythe journey here!

Patrick Smythe is a former Northern Irish policeman who

after suffering an amputation after a bomb blast, takes to the sea between the west coast of Scotland and his homeland to ply his trade as a private investigator. Join Paddy as he tries to work to his own ethics while knowing how to bend the rules he once enforced. Working from his beloved motorboat 'Craigantlet', Paddy decides to rescue a drug mule in this short story from the pen of G R Jordan.

Join G R Jordan's monthly newsletter about forthcoming releases and special writings for his tribe of avid readers and then receive your free Patrick Smythe short story.

Go to https://bit.ly/PatrickSmythe for your Patrick Smythe journey to start!

About the Author

GR Jordan is a self-published author who finally decided at forty that in order to have an enjoyable lifestyle, his creative beast within would have to be unleashed. His books mirror that conflict in life where acts of decency contend with self-promotion, goodness stares in horror at evil, and kindness blindsides us when we at our worst. Corrupting our world with his parade of wondrous and horrific characters, he highlights everyday tensions with fresh eyes whilst taking his methodical, intelligent mainstays on a roller-coaster ride of dilemmas, all the while suffering the banter of their provocative sidekicks.

A graduate of Loughborough University where he masqueraded as a chemical engineer but ultimately played American football, Gary had worked at changing the shape of cereal flakes and pulled a pallet truck for a living. Watching vegetables freeze at -40'C was another career highlight and he was also one of the Scottish Highlands "blind" air traffic controllers.

These days he has graduated to answering a telephone to people in trouble before telephoning other people to sort it out.

Having flirted with most places in the UK, he is now based in the Isle of Lewis in Scotland where his free time is spent between raising a young family with his wife, writing, figuring out how to work a loom and caring for a small flock of chickens. Luckily, his writing is influenced by his varied work and life experience as the chickens have not been the poetical inspiration he had hoped for!

You can connect with me on:

🌐 https://grjordan.com

f https://facebook.com/carpetlessleprechaun

Subscribe to my newsletter:

✉ https://bit.ly/PatrickSmythe

Also by G R Jordan

G R Jordan writes across multiple genres including crime, dark and action adventure fantasy, feel good fantasy, mystery thriller and horror fantasy. Below is a selection of his work. Whilst all books are available across online stores, signed copies are available at his personal shop.

Anti-social Behaviour (A Highlands & Islands Detective Thriller #20)
https://grjordan.com/product/antisocial-behaviour
A youth is found dead at a children's playpark. A stolen car burnt out with the joyriders inside. Can Macleod discover the avenging angel brutally restoring the highland's peace and quiet?

When a spate of deaths indicating teenagers as targets sends Macleod and McGrath into a very public hunt for killer, they must walk in view of the hottest debate of the day. But when Hope believes she sees an angle that points the blame at those who responsible for the nation's safety, Macleod must trust his Sergeant's instincts while dodging a career ending bullet.

It was all easier back in the day, or was it?

The Man Everyone Wanted (A Kirsten Stewart Thriller #7)
https://grjordan.com/product/the-man-everyone-wanted
A foreign agent goes rogue on Scottish soil. A city centre bloodbath shows the stakes at play. Can Kirsten secure the agent amidst a plethora of deadly friends and enemies?

When a shootout in the centre of Inverness ends in a mass of foreign bodies, Anna Hunt tasks recently recovered Kirsten Stewart with finding out why? When the trail leads to an agent who holds the key to a country's invasion, Kirsten must tread between friend and foe to bring the plans to light and stop a war. Will Kirsten prevail and avoid a myriad of friendly fire in the process?

You can always take a bullet for anyone's agenda!

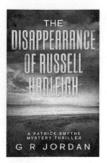

The Disappearance of Russell Hadleigh (Patrick Smythe Book 1)
https://grjordan.com/product/the-disappearance-of-russell-hadleigh
A retired judge fails to meet his golf partner. His wife calls for help while running a fantasy play ring. When Russians start co-opting into a fairly-traded clothing brand, can Paddy untangle the strands before the bodies start littering the golf course?

In his first full novel, Patrick Smythe, the single-armed former policeman, must infiltrate the golfing social scene to discover the fate of his client's husband. Assisted by a young starlet of the greens, Paddy tries to understand just who bears a grudge and who likes to play in the rough, culminating in a high stakes showdown where lives are hanging by the reaction of a moment. If you love pacey action, suspicious motives and devious characters, then Paddy Smythe operates amongst your kind of people.

Love is a matter of taste but money always demands more of its suitor.

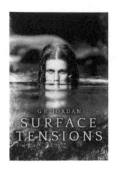

Surface Tensions (Island Adventures Book 1)
https://grjordan.com/product/surface-tensions
Mermaids sighted near a Scottish island. A town exploding in anger and distrust. And Donald's got to get the sexiest fish in town, back in the water.

"Surface Tensions" is the first story in a series of Island adventures from the pen of G R Jordan. If you love comic moments, cosy adventures and light fantasy action, then you'll love these tales with a twist. Get the book that amazon readers said, "perfectly captures life in the Scottish Hebrides" and that explores "human nature at its best and worst".

Something's stirring the water!

Corpse Reviver (A Contessa Munroe Mystery #1)
https://grjordan.com/product/corspe-reviver
A widowed Contessa flees to the northern waters in search of adventure. An entrepreneur dies on an ice pack excursion. But when the victim starts moonlighting from his locked cabin, can the Contessa uncover the true mystery of his death?

Catriona Cullodena Munroe, widow of the late Count de Los Palermo, has fled the family home, avoiding the scramble for title and land. As she searches for the life she always wanted, the Contessa, in the company of the autistic and rejected Tiff, must solve the mystery of a man who just won't let his business go.

Corpse Reviver is the first murder mystery involving the formidable and sometimes downright rude lady of leisure and her straight talking niece. Bonded by blood, and thrown together by fate, join this pair of thrill seekers as they realise that flirting with danger brings a price to pay.

Lightning Source UK Ltd.
Milton Keynes UK
UKHW010746130622
404345UK00001B/254

9 781914 073939